Taming the Willful Miss Roberts

Maryse Dawson

Published by Maryse Dawson, 2024.

TAMING THE WILLFUL MISS ROBERTS

First edition. March 6, 2024.

ISBN: 979-8230103370

Written by Maryse Dawson.

Table of Contents

Chapter One

Woolwich, London, 1877

Lord Oliver Berkeley looked out of the small office window overlooking the Thames. It was the middle of winter and in parts, the long meandering river showed signs of freezing, revealing how cold the air temperature was. He had never liked winter. Hated the snow even more. He glanced down to the street below, his lip curling as he looked at the churned up sludge, softly illuminated by the gas lamps.

His thoughts were interrupted by his colleague entering the room. Clarence Roberts had only recently joined his practice and he was proving to be a great asset to him. Oliver was a lawyer and due to his success he found he had far too many cases to deal with. So he had set to finding someone to help ease the burden.

It didn't take long before Clarence approached him and being as highly qualified as he was himself and finding him a highly affable fellow, he had hired him on the spot.

That had been a month ago and Oliver's workload had lessened immeasurably.

"You have returned early." Oliver remarked, looking at him. "Did something happen?"

Clarence dumped a big folder on the desk and loosened his cravat. "Indeed. Lord Huntingdon fell ill during our meeting. So I will have to return when he is recovered."

"He is not the most healthy of men." Oliver noted, picturing his ruddy face due to drinking copious amounts of alcohol.

"Indeed, he is not." Clarence walked over to a small cabinet and withdrew a bottle of rum. "I quite fancy a snifter. How about you?"

Oliver shook his head. "No, I must be off home."

"Are you still coming to the wedding tomorrow? Mother wants to know how many guest bedrooms to prepare. With this perishing cold, we will need many fires burning in their hearths!"

"Of course. I was quite honoured that you invited me in the first place. I must say though, it is an unusual time of year to get married."

Clarence laughed, "I think my sister, Florence, wants to get hitched as soon as possible. She is twenty-eight and now she has finally fallen in love, she has no intention of letting her beau escape."

Oliver smiled. "Do you like your future brother-in-law?"

"I have met him twice and I can honestly say, he seems to be a rather likeable chap. You will find out for yourself tomorrow. In fact, I am quite looking forward to introducing you to my family. They have asked many questions about you, so it will satiate their curiosity."

"It will indeed." He walked over to the coat stand. "I will leave you to lock up. See you tomorrow." He shrugged on his long coat and grabbing his hat from the stand, he left for home.

Montgomery was already waiting for him outside, the carriage door open and the steps down. "Bit cold, isn't it, m'lord?"

"You could say that."

He stepped inside and in a few moments, the carriage was rattling along the cobblestone roads towards home.

—⟨∞⟩—

*E*vesham Manor, Kent

The grand house, set in several acres of land, was a hive of activity as everyone played their part to make sure everything would look splendid for the wedding celebrations that afternoon.

Much to her annoyance, Amelia Roberts had been woken up at the crack of dawn to help out. She had been having such a lovely dream as well. But her mother had insisted she make some effort telling her that when her time came, wouldn't she expect everyone to help out?

Amelia pulled a face at the thought. She was younger than her sister, Florence by five years and at twenty-three she hoped that her wedding day was a long way off. She loved her independence and so far hadn't been introduced to anyone that she liked, let alone wanted to marry. They were either too priggish or too boring and not one of them had set her pulse racing. So no, the longer she could keep off such an event, the better.

She had rolled her eyes and reluctantly set to helping out with the flower displays. She had never been any good at arranging flowers and it soon showed when her mother began tutting and repositioning all she had done. She soon packed her off to the dining room hoping that tying ribbons wouldn't be beyond her capabilities.

But Amelia only had one thing in mind and that was to make herself scarce. She made certain her mother was out of sight and then headed straight back up to her bedroom to certain solitude.

Throwing herself on the bed, she lay on her front and thought about her sister. She loved Florence and was truly happy that she was getting married but she would miss her when she left. Her bottom lip pouted with self-pity. They had always done a lot together, riding, reading, even embroidery on the occasions Florence could get Amelia to take part. She laughed to herself as she acknowledged her lack of expertise where that particular task was concerned. She just had to accept that she would never be good at needlework. Besides, that's what servants were for.

She rolled on her back and looked up at the patterned ceiling, wondering who was going to be at the wedding. She knew her dear friend, Cora Spencer was going to attend so that would make for a fun evening and also there would be certain relatives attending. She grimaced as a vision of her Aunt Hortensia sprang to mind. She would have to try and stay out of her way, she could bore one half to death!

Her brother, Clarence had said he had invited his new employer. She hadn't had much chance to talk with Clarence since he had taken up the new position in Woolwich so she had no idea what the man looked like. She'd bet he was a crusty old dullard with no sense of humour. She smiled wickedly.

Her thoughts returned to her sister's imminent departure. As sad as it was, at least she could visit her at her new house. Now there was an exciting thought. She liked Albert Portman, her soon to be brother-in-law, so she was certain he would have no objection to her staying every now and then. Oh yes, that was a splendid idea. It perked her up no end.

Rising from the bed, she wandered over to the window. The snow was still quite thick on the ground and if it wasn't for the constantly lit hearths, the house would be like an ice cave. Thankfully, they had a team of servants that kept them stoked and constantly churning out heat.

A knock on the door broke her out of her reverie and she immediately stiffened. Oh lord! If her mother found her in here, she'd be in no end of trouble. Diving under the bed, she kept quiet and peered at the bottom of the door to see if it would open. It did.

Soon a pair of eyes were staring back at her. It was her maid, Anna. "Mistress Amelia! Whatever are you doing under there?" She tutted loudly. "Your Mama has been looking for you everywhere!"

"Close the door! *Close the door!*" Amelia whispered urgently. "Are you deliberately trying to get me in trouble!" She hissed angrily.

Anna darted back and shut the door before returning. "If your Mama finds you in here, you are going to be in so much trouble!"

"Well, she isn't, is she?" Amelia exclaimed, scrabbling out from beneath the bed. Anna, set about neatening Amelia's skirts, brushing the fabric down with her hands.

"You shouldn't be getting into trouble on your sister's wedding day. Goodness me!"

Amelia would reprimand most servants but Anna had been with her since birth, so she was almost like a second mother and she was used to her ways . Still, she slapped her hands away. "Go and tell Mama that you cannot find me." Anna shot her a look full of disapproval so Amelia added sweetly, "Please?"

Anna rolled her eyes. "Very well, just this once. But if I were you, I'd go back down and make yourself useful, else she'll tell your father... and you don't want that, do you?"

Amelia shook her head. No, she didn't! Her father was a very strict man and she rarely got away with anything. He would certainly punish her. Last time, he had sent her off to stay with Aunt Hortensia for a week. Good lord. She didn't want to experience that again!

She waited a few minutes for Anna to leave and then reluctantly went back downstairs. By the time her mother found her, she was helping organise the decorations on the long dining table.

"Oh, there you are!" Her mother said, relieved to finally get hold of her.

"Oh? Did you wish to speak with me, Mama?" She asked, her eyes wide expressing such innocence that her mother immediately was unsure whether she was guilty of shunning her chores or not.

Her mother frowned for a second before replying, "No, I suppose it doesn't matter." She looked to the table and her attention was quickly diverted when she saw a napkin wrongly folded. "Oh, do I have to do everything myself!"

Amelia hid a smile. Thankfully, she had neatly avoided a reprimand. She followed her mother and resigned herself to the task at hand.

─ ⚬ ─

Oliver arrived at Evesham Manor in plenty of time for the ceremony and entering the wrought iron gates, he cautiously urged his horse along the snow laden driveway towards the elegant country mansion, nestling amidst snow covered bushes and tall fir trees.

It was a truly beautiful house, set atop a gentle hill, its grey stone walls looking out over a soft rolling landscape. Tall turrets stood at each corner of the three-story structure, with gabled windows peering out from under pointed archways.

He estimated it to have at least eighteen or twenty bedrooms. It made his own house, Bedford Hall, with only ten bedrooms look small in comparison.

Reaching the front of the house, he was quickly greeted by a stable hand. "Good afternoon, Sir."

Oliver dismounted and handed his horse Monson into the safekeeping of Evesham Manor's stables and then quickly walked up the ornate stone steps to the house. A butler opened the massive oak door the minute he arrived, he didn't even have to raise his hand to the polished brass knocker before he was ushered inside.

"Good day, Sir. Welcome to Evesham Manor. Allow me to take your hat and overcoat. May I have your name?"

"Lord Oliver Berkeley of Bedford Hall." He removed his hat and the butler helped him off with his heavy overcoat, brushing it down with his hands.

"I shall have your luggage taken to your room, m'lord."

The butler was pleasant but struck him as a very serious fellow. The man clicked his fingers and in an instant a young lad appeared. "To the green room." He said without preamble, pointing to Oliver's carpet bag. The boy was gone in a thrice. "My name is Simmons, I am the butler here. If you need anything do let me know. Now, if you would follow me, m'lord."

He was led into a large parlour where several people were already gathered. Clarence spotted him at once and with a broad smile on his face, strode over to him. "Lord Oliver! I am so glad you could make it. Come, let me introduce you to everyone."

He was quickly introduced to his parents and several friends and other relatives before Clarence led him away to show him the rest of the house and the room in which he would be staying.

Amelia looked at herself in the mirror and smiled happily. Her new dress was so beautiful and simply perfect for her sister's wedding. It was white silk, trimmed with lilac and white lace and adorned with small flowers in the same colours. Anna had styled her hair with long separate coils at the back, the front swept off her face and the sides pinned back neatly. With some pretty lilac combs and a fashionable lilac shawl she was finally ready to make an appearance.

"Oh, you do look beautiful, mistress Amelia."

"Thank you, Anna."

A knock came on the door and Anna walked over to open it. It was her friend, Cora. A smile split her face when she saw how beautiful Amelia looked. "Oh, my!" she said, walking over, "I adore your dress!"

"Do you truly? Miss Foster made it for me. She is such a wonderful seamstress."

"Oh, the one from Madame Floren's Boutique?"

Amelia nodded and then looked her friend up and down. "You look beautiful too, Cora. The green suits your eyes." Cora had stunning green eyes and a mop of bright red hair which her maid always had terrible trouble taming. But she had managed it today for it was neatly fashioned into a bun at the nape of her neck with little green flower clips at the sides.

"I shall leave you together to chat. The ceremony will begin in an hour, so I suggest you two remain here and out of trouble." Anna breezed out of the room before Amelia could reply, leaving her staring at the door with her lips pursed.

"What does she mean? We rarely get into trouble." Cora huffed.

Amelia bit her bottom lip and then laughed. "You might not but I have a tendency to. Talking of which, I snaffled something from Clarence's room today. Do you want to see?"

Cora's eyes widened. "What is it?"

Amelia walked over to her wardrobe and opening the door, reached under a pile of blankets and brought out a small slingshot. She held it up with a wicked grin on her face. "He used to use this when he was little. I remember it."

Cora walked over and took it out of her hands, inspecting it and then pulling back the thin rope. "Have you got any missiles?"

Amelia opened a little bag and pulled out several small balls made of wood. She took the slingshot off Cora, loaded it with a small ball and took aim at the bed. It hit the target and bounced off onto the floor.

"Oh, it's quite powerful. Can I have a go?"

Cora failed miserably on her first attempt but managed the second. "We need a longer range, I want to see how far it will travel."

Amelia grinned and opening the bedroom door looked left and right along the long corridor. "No one's about, come on!"

They crept out into the corridor and Amelia loaded another ball, held the sling shot up and took aim towards the other end. Just as she released her hand, two men appeared at the top of the stairs in the direct path of the oncoming missile.

Cora clapped a hand to her mouth and her eyes wide, dove straight back into Amelia's bedroom. Amelia wasn't so quick and was just in time to see the wooden ball make contact with one of the men. It hit his shoulder and pinged off. She didn't waste any time hanging about. Rushing into her bedroom she slammed the door and was just about to turn the key, when the door was pushed roughly inward.

Her brother stood there, eyes blazing. "What the hell do you think you are doing?"

Amelia raised her chin defiantly. "Nothing!" Her hands were behind her back, holding the sling hook tightly. She glanced at Cora, who had a horrified expression and was cowering on the edge of the bed. To protect her friend, she decided she would take the sole blame for what had happened. She was used to getting into trouble, her friend was not.

Clarence shook his head and turning her around, ripped the sling hook out of her hands. He held it up in front of her face. "Now tell me you weren't up to anything?"

She tightened her lips angrily and then retorted. "I was just having a little fun. I wanted to show Cora how far the ball went. I didn't know you were going to turn up at that precise moment!"

"You just hit Lord Berkeley directly on his shoulder - what if you had hit his face? What if that ball had gone into his eye! He could have been blinded!"

"You make it sound like it was deliberate!" Amelia responded hotly, her voice rising. "I would never do that to someone on purpose."

Oliver stood out in the hallway listening to the conversation and decided to intervene before it got out of hand. Today was supposed to be a day of happiness and he could see matters escalating quickly if he didn't step in.

He moved forward into the doorway and looked over Clarence's shoulders at the girl concerned. She was a petite little thing with gorgeous golden blonde hair but even though she was stunningly beautiful he knew without a shadow of a doubt that she was trouble with a capital T.

Her eyes flashed fire and she looked more concerned with being caught out than what she had actually done. He stepped into her vision, to the side of Clarence and fixed her with a stern look. "I think, Miss, that you owe me an apology."

Her eyes of violet blue shot to his and he saw in their depths a hint of annoyance. She appeared to be a precocious little madam and was having a damned hard time trying to hide it. She was a handful indeed but nothing that a good bottom warming wouldn't fail to curb. His hand itched to hitch up her skirts, turn her over his knee and administer several swats.

Clarence folded his arms and glared at her. "Well?"

Oliver watched as she clasped her hands together in front of her and then she managed to utter an apology, of sorts.

"Please forgive me, Lord Berkeley. I didn't mean for the ball to hit you."

Even though she was saying the words, he knew that she most definitely didn't mean it. Her whole demeanour was one of sassy impudence.

"I will accept your apology on this occasion but I trust it won't happen again."

* * *

Amelia's eyes flashed and she felt like saying, *or what?* But she managed to keep quiet. Just. She eyed him carefully. He held a hint of sternness that she had only previously seen in her father. A certain strength of character that brooked no disobedience or silliness. Of which she possessed copious amounts of both.

He was taller than her brother and had wavy dark hair with eyes of hazel brown. And, even though she hated to admit it, he was very handsome. Very handsome indeed. She pulled her gaze away and looked at her brother.

Clarence turned the slingshot over in his hands and then said, "And don't ever go snooping around in my bedroom again." She went to speak and he raised his hand. "Don't even think about lying! You know very well this was in my drawer. If you do so again, I will tell father. It is that simple."

Amelia huffed in response and folded her arms. That was a direct threat and a dire one. Eugh.

"Well, I suppose I should introduce you two." Clarence said and turning to Oliver said, "I know it is a trifle late but may I introduce my youngest sister, Miss Amelia Roberts and her friend Miss Cora Spencer."

Amelia watched as Lord Berkeley looked slightly taken aback and he replied, "*This* is your sister?"

"And what do you mean by that remark, my lord?" Amelia huffed.

She saw him raise an eyebrow and without preamble he said. "I would have thought that someone of your upbringing would be a little less... wild."

Clarence immediately guffawed, "Wild! Well said, Lord Oliver."

"Well said?!" Amelia gasped. "He cannot speak to me like that!"

"He just did and if you hadn't of shot him with a slingshot then he would have no cause. But you did and he does." Clarence explained.

Amelia's temper came to the fore and she put her hand on the door knob. "I want both of you to leave!"

"We intend to," Clarence said and turning to Cora, nodded politely before he walked out of the room.

Oliver smiled at Cora showing even white teeth and for a moment Amelia was speechless. He looked even more handsome when he wasn't frowning. Good lord! However, his expression changed when he moved his gaze onto Amelia. Something in his eyes made her shiver and she quickly realised he was a dangerous man to cross. Clarence's boss wasn't the crusty old man she thought he would be! Oh, no indeed.

When the door closed behind them, Amelia threw herself on the bed, making the mattress bounce and Cora leaned over to look at her, her face flushed. "Oh, my, Amelia. What a debacle!"

"Why did they have to arrive precisely at that moment?" She huffed.

"At least no one was harmed," Cora added, "Although I have never seen your brother angry like that before."

Amelia gave a wry smile, "I have on many an occasion."

"I shouldn't like to get on his bad side. I think you are very brave, Amelia."

"Maybe." She sat up and glanced down at her dress. "I think you and I should neaten ourselves a little before returning downstairs. Mama will have a fit if she sees me with my hair out of place."

Cora grinned, "I agree. Come and sit by the dressing table and I will attend you."

Whilst Cora repinned the few strands of hair that had escaped their confines, Amelia looked at her reflection. Was she wild? She frowned. If, by wild, he meant she had a free spirit then yes, she was a little. But that was no concern of his!

One thing, however, *was* her concern and that was making sure she stayed out of the ogres way during the upcoming celebrations. She had no wish to speak to a man that had called her wild!

Chapter Two

The wedding was held in the small chapel on Evesham Manor's estate, and before long, a very happy and serene Florence Roberts became Mrs. Albert Portman. The wedding guests were quickly ushered back to the warm house and were soon settled at the gloriously decorated long table in the grand dining room with the newly married couple seated at the head.

Food started arriving, course by course with many glasses raised to wish the happy couple a long and prosperous life together.

Amelia had never seen her sister look so happy and it heartened her to see. She truly deserved a happy union and so far, Albert had proved himself worthy of her sister's devotion. She took another sip of her champagne and looked around the table.

Much to her annoyance, she had found herself seated directly opposite Lord Berkeley of all people. She had tried to keep her gaze diverted but every now and then she found they were drawn to him and much to her chagrin, she had found that each time, he was already looking at her. But rather than look away, he held her gaze.

Her face flushing, she had drunk just a little more than she should have and already her head felt a little fuzzy and light. But it was fun.

Cora was next to her and was having just as good a time as she was. In fact, she seemed to be talking to her brother quite a lot who was seated next to Lord Berkeley on the opposite side.

Amelia wondered if she liked Clarence. He was quite handsome but he was also a pig. But maybe that was just an attitude kept especially for her? She sniggered and took another sip of the sparkling champagne, wrinkling her nose when the tiny bubbles tickled her skin.

"You would do well to slow your intake, Miss Roberts. The champagne can be quite intoxicating."

Amelia looked across at Lord Berkeley as he spoke and with a hint of defiance in her eyes, retorted, "Lord Berkeley, although I thank you for your concern, please do not presume to tell me what I can and cannot do."

She held his gaze for a moment and then took a long draught to mock him, licking her lips appreciatively at the heady beverage. She watched in fascination when his jaw tightened with disapproval and was delighted to find that it gave her a lot of satisfaction. He may have had the upper hand earlier but not now.

She shot him a wicked smile before downing the rest and raising her finger for another. Oh yes, she decided, she would have great fun in defying Lord Berkeley at every single turn.

⎯⎯ ⁐ ⎯⎯

With the meal finished, most of the guests retired to their rooms for a little respite and also to change into their evening attire if they wished. The household staff scurried about clearing the remnants of the lavish meal from the long tables under the watchful eye of Simmons, for once that was done they had the hall to prepare for the evening festivities. Time was of the essence. When no crumb remained, the wooden table was polished to a perfect sheen and the staff appointed to the large hall where they set about the next preparations.

Amelia and Cora had opted to go to the library. Both loved reading and Amelia's father had recently acquired some new books so she couldn't wait to share them with her friend.

Chattering excitedly, they entered the large room and headed over to one of the large bookshelves. There were many tall shelves holding books of every variety. From novels to encyclopedias, maps to cookery books. It was a vast collection, hence the size of the room.

"Papa said he had several new books on poems. Oh, and one on wolves. I might need to read that so I know how to deal with Lord Berkeley!"

Cora's eyes widened and she spluttered, "Amelia, hush! Someone might hear you!"

"Pffff! I care not." She looked around and spread her arms wide. "There is no one here but us two. You worry far too much."

Suddenly, someone coughed and both girls froze. Amelia's eyes widened and she clapped a hand over her mouth. Who the devil was that?

Finding the situation a lot funnier than she should, mainly because she had always had a wicked sense of humour, she grabbed Cora's hand and quickly ushered her behind one of the tall shelving units, giggling quietly.

"Do you think they heard us?" Cora whispered.

"I don't think so, at least I hope not." She sniggered. "Where on earth were they hiding?"

"I told you to be careful!" Cora said, in a worried tone.

Amelia quietened her breathing and listened hard. She couldn't hear anything so taking a risk, she peered out and nearly jumped out of her skin when she found someone standing right in front of her. She swallowed hard and looked up to find Lord Berkeley staring down at her. She couldn't quite fathom his expression. Was he annoyed? Angry? It was hard to tell.

"Miss Roberts. What good fortune that I find you here." His deep voice broke the silence.

"Oh?" Amelia eyed him cautiously.

"Indeed it is. May I speak with you? Do excuse us, Miss Spencer." He didn't wait for Cora's reply but simply took Amelia's hand and led her over towards the fireplace. She found herself obeying him silently and she wasn't sure why. Maybe it was his manner - it brooked no refusal.

He dropped his hand and stared down at her. "I wondered if you would honour me with a dance this evening."

She frowned. This was an unexpected turn of events. "You wish to dance with me?"

He nodded.

Maybe he hadn't heard what she said after all. Thank the lord. She eyed him shrewdly wondering why he would want to dance with her and then, tilting her head, she said, "Surely I am too *wild* to choose as a dance partner."

The corner of his mouth twitched with mirth and he leaned his face near to hers. His eyes were so close she could see flecks of gold in their hazel depths. It was a little disconcerting and she felt her pulse begin to race at his close proximity.

"A perfect choice for a wolf I believe!"

Her face flushed red at being caught out and to hide her guilt, she went on the attack. Raising her chin defiantly, she snapped, "I am uncertain yet whom I wish to dance with."

"You *will* dance with me." He seemed so assured that she was suddenly at a loss for words. She had never met anyone like him. Most people were quite easy to manipulate but not so, Lord Berkeley it would seem.

Nodding politely, he exited the room without another word. As soon as he had gone, Cora rushed over from the other side of the room, her eyes wide with curiosity. "What did he say? Did he hear you refer to him as a wolf?"

Amelia nodded, still wondering why her stomach was doing somersaults. Why was he having such an affect on her? It must be the champagne she had drank during the meal. She tried to shake off the feeling and explained to Cora that Lord Berkeley wished to dance with her tonight.

"He does?" She grabbed her hand, "Then he must have fallen for you! Surely?"

Amelia raised an eyebrow. "Fallen for me? In one day?" She shook her head dismissively. "Besides, so what if he has? I have to feel the same for anything to progress and I don't! He is far too... too overbearing!"

As soon as she spoke the words, she knew she was lying. He was the first man to set her pulse racing and her heart aflutter. But she would keep that a secret for now - she didn't even want to admit it to herself let alone anyone else.

The dance began with a formal procession, led by the bride and groom, gracefully gliding across the dance floor, their hands entwined and their happiness clear to see. They looked marvellous together and Amelia couldn't help but smile.

She noted her mother had a tear in her eye and even her father didn't look quite as stern as usual. Now, that was something to bear witness to indeed.

The next dance of the evening was the waltz and both Cora and Amelia found themselves whisked onto the dance floor by two of Albert Portman's friends. Cora's was rather dashing but Amelia's partner had two left feet and she couldn't wait for the music to end. She was surprised they hadn't fallen into another couple and caused havoc. Smiling politely, she quickly departed his company towards the refreshment area and notably the large bowl of delicious punch she had eyed earlier.

She only had time to take two sips before Lord Berkeley appeared in front of her.

"I believe you promised me a dance." He said, taking the cup from her hands.

She shook her head, "No, I didn't. You...!"

She didn't get to finish the rest of her sentence before he was leading her away. She thought about protesting and then realised it would just leave room for a tattle tales to start their idle gossip. Something she had no time for.

So reluctantly, she allowed him to lead her onto the dance floor. He placed his large hand firmly on her waist and she rested her gloved hand delicately on his shoulders - very broad and very masculine shoulders. She swallowed hard. What was wrong with her? She shouldn't be thinking like this, the man was far too authoritarian for her taste.

The music swelled, and he led her effortlessly across the floor in perfect synchrony, their movements as smooth as silk. It was as though they were made for each other and it was truly delightful. Especially after her previous dance partner.

She looked up at him in wonderment, her eyes sparkling and was amazed to see that in those hazel depths was a desire that mirrored her own.

Shocked she looked away, her teeth pulling her bottom lip in whilst she thought upon the situation. This was all very sudden and hard to contemplate. There was no denying her attraction to the formidable man but would she wish to have a suitor like him?

By the time the lively tune came to its conclusion, Amelia found herself quite breathless, though she couldn't say if it was from the exertion of the dance or the dizzying effect of her growing feelings for her handsome dance partner.

Lord Berkeley escorted her from the floor and sweeping into a low bow, he pressed a fleeting kiss to her gloved knuckles. "You dance divinely, Miss Roberts."

With a parting smile, he went to join her brother in lively discussion with her father across the hall.

Cora touched her arm and looking in Lord Berkeley's direction remarked, "He is very dashing, Amelia and watching the two of you dance together... oh my! He would make a most suitable husband for you."

Amelia grabbed her fan and began fanning her hot cheeks. "Cora, today is the first time I have met him and to be perfectly honest, I am not even sure that I like him." She stared across the hall and found herself admiring his tall, strong figure. Of course, he was undeniably handsome but he had the audacity to call her wild!

"I think he likes you."

Amelia snapped her fan closed and said to her friend, "We cannot be certain of that. He has a very brooding presence and I am not sure whether I like it or not. Anyway, what gives you reason to think that he likes me?"

"Oh, I don't know. Maybe it's the look in his eyes. I just feel there is something between you."

Amelia didn't know what she thought and reaching behind Cora, she picked her drink up from the table. "One thing I do know is that tonight my intention is to have a wonderful time and have many dance partners!" She raised her glass and closed her eyes at the sweet and fruity aroma wafting up from the punch. Oh, yes, she intended to have a few of these tonight and dance until her feet could take no more.

Her eyes twinkling with devilment she looked across the room to find Lord Berkeley staring at her, a disapproving frown on his forehead. Raising her glass in a toast, she took another sip and deliberately turned her back. Fie on him and his judgemental looks!

An hour later, Amelia and Cora were quite exhausted from all the dancing, their faces flushed with exhilaration and satisfaction. They had just danced a rather energetic quadrille and were both ready for a break.

Cora giggled and sliding her arm through Amelia's said, "Did you see Mr. Jackson's face? I have never seen it so red. I think perhaps that the quadrille was a little too much for him."

Amelia gave an unladylike snort and quickly placed a hand over her mouth, before spluttering, "I thought he was going to have a funny turn."

They reached one of the long tables at the side of the room and Amelia held her hand out for a cup of punch. A large hand immediately settled over hers and shocked she turned around to find Lord Berkeley standing beside her.

"I think you have had quite enough for one evening, Miss Roberts. I would suggest a refreshing glass of water."

Amelia blinked quickly, did she just hear him correctly? She stared at him and trying to control her temper, she said sharply, "I beg your pardon?"

"You heard me very well, Miss Roberts."

Cora's eyes were darting around in her head, wondering what to do and she said quietly, "We have only had a couple of drinks, my Lord. We are not inebriated."

"Miss Spencer, you may not be but Miss Roberts has had far too much. Your brother was discussing it with me just now and asked me to come and intervene."

Amelia's face flushed with anger. "You were both discussing me?"

He nodded, not in the least perturbed. "Indeed. Clarence was going to come himself but one of his friends is leaving, so he wanted to see him off safely."

Amelia could feel her hand begin to shake as her anger threatened to overwhelm her. "So, I am not allowed to enjoy myself? I have to watch my consumption of alcohol because my brother thinks I am inebriated. Is that correct?"

Lord Berkeley's mouth twitched with mirth and he nodded, adding, "And he said that if you defy him, he will tell your father."

"Why the...!"

"Please refrain from expletives, Miss Roberts. Remember where you are!"

Her eyes narrowing, she took hold of her friend's hand and glaring up at Lord Berkeley, she hissed, "Come Cora, I have no wish to stay in this gentleman's presence any longer!" And with a swish of skirts, she led Cora across the room and out into the hallway. The further away she was from Lord Berkeley the better!

A little while later and safely ensconced in the games room, Amelia took a sip of the velvety smooth punch and grinned at Cora.

"Is this not better than having our fun curtailed by an infuriating ogre?"

Cora giggled quietly and leaned her head back against the plush sofa. Several men were playing billiards at the other end of the room, the small balls making a loud click as they knocked against each other. In another corner, several tables were set up for cards and both men and women were engrossed in their quest to win some money.

Cora and Amelia were thankfully left undisturbed and they found it a nice respite from the busy dance hall. Having time to think, Amelia focussed on Lord Berkeley. He had not only shown his disapproval for her drinking at the dinner table but also later. And to think that he and her brother had been talking about her like that! Goodness. You'd have thought they had better things to discuss.

Perhaps Lord Berkeley needed something else to focus on? In fact, she had just the thing, she thought cunningly and she would put her plan into action when she retired to her bedroom. She knew that Lord Berkeley was staying in the green room, not far from hers, so a quick nip in and out with no one noticing would be easy to execute. A little revenge on the irksome man, would finish off her day perfectly!

Grinning, she finished her drink and both girls returned to the ball room for the last dance and to see the newly married couple off to the west wing of the house where they would have privacy for their first night together.

Amelia chose to retire just after midnight, when several guests had already left, either by carriage or if they were staying at Evesham had retired to their allotted bedrooms. Cora had accompanied her parents back to their own house as they preferred their own home comforts.

Amelia entered her bedroom and saw that as usual, her bed covers had been turned down and the candles lit by the servants, giving off a lovely warm glow. It looked so inviting that she thought of just going to bed but her quest for vengeance was too strong.

Walking over to her chest of drawers, she opened the bottom one and rummaged around beneath the clothing to find a small book. She bit her lip and stopped for a second. Was she truly going to go through with this? What if Lord Berkeley discovered her trickery?

She shook her head. He couldn't and wouldn't. She opened the book and within the pages was a small envelope of powder. Itching powder!

She had been saving it to use on Clarence for a prank but this opportunity was far more worthy. It was a peculiar concoction that she had acquired from her cousin, Thomas. He had told her that it contained a mixture of dried nettles, prickly thistles and finely ground mustard seeds. Together these elements created a substance that, when applied to the skin or clothing, would trigger an intense and persistent itching sensation.

Perfect for an overbearing tyrant!

Clutching the little envelope in her hands, she waited impatiently for the noise in the corridor to quieten down before even thinking about doing her dastardly deed. She could still hear people walking past, some a little louder than others.

Finally, everything quietened, so her heart in her mouth, Amelia opened her bedroom door and peered out. The coast was clear. Stepping out into the corridor, she stealthily made her way to the green room, keeping her body slightly hunched to avoid detection.

Reaching his room, she placed her ear against the door and listened hard. There was nothing but silence so taking a deep breath, she grasped the handle and turned it slowly and cautiously. Opening the door a fraction she peered inside. She had no idea what she was going to say if he was there. But thankfully he wasn't. So as quick as lightning she stepped inside, closing the door behind her.

Now she was inside, she knew she had to act fast. So heading towards his wardrobe she opened the heavy door to see which clothes were hanging up. There was a waistcoat, a jacket, a shirt and a pair of trousers. She tapped a fingernail on her bottom lip wondering which one would be best.

It was then that her gaze fell upon an open carpet bag and she immediately knew where she was going to put the powder. His nightshirt! She could see it neatly folded within the bag so quickly, she opened the envelope and sprinkled some of the powder inside the folds.

Suddenly, she became aware of footsteps in the corridor. What if it was Lord Berkeley? Oh lord! She froze and then to her horror, they stopped right outside his room. She didn't waste a second.

Clambering inside, she closed the door and hid in the darkness. The smell of aged wood and fabric assailed her senses and in the confined space, her fear threatened to overwhelm her. What if he should discover her? What would he do? She couldn't stay there all night!

She closed her eyes tightly, hoping it was someone else walking past but to her dismay she heard the door open and someone strode in, closing the door behind them. Perhaps it was a servant? But then would they close the door after them? She winced, concluding that no, they wouldn't.

She remained still and kept her breathing shallow but her heart was racing with fear and trepidation. The sound of footsteps drew nearer and her breath caught in her throat. Time seemed to stand still as she looked in fascination at the doorknob when it started to turn.

Oh, lord!

Suddenly the wardrobe door opened and she found herself face to face with Lord Berkeley and not only that but he was dressed in just his trousers with his chest bare. His very muscular, manly chest!

Amelia gasped and tried to clamber out and push past him but too late, he had her captured.

Holding her arm in a tight grip, he growled, "What the devil are you doing in my wardrobe?"

Chapter Three

Oliver couldn't believe what he was seeing but the proof was standing before him. Miss Roberts stared back at him with a mixture of guilt and defiance.

"I will ask you again. What are you doing in here?" he demanded, loosening his grip but still keeping hold of her.

She fidgeted nervously, "I was... errr... looking for our... cat."

"A cat?"

She raised her chin. "Yes, our cat. One of the servants mentioned that she came into your room, so I thought I should retrieve her. I didn't want your sleep disturbed."

"I see." He nodded his head, knowing she was lying but still unsure as to why she was in his room. Something didn't add up. And he would reason she was up to no good, rather than trying to locate a cat.

"So, where is this cat?" he asked.

"She wasn't here."

"Of course she wasn't." He looked behind her at the wardrobe. "And in the process of looking for this cat, you accidentally shut yourself in the wardrobe?"

"Well, you scared me so I hid."

He couldn't resist laughing at her. "Do you truly think I am going to believe any of what you just said?"

"Yes!"

It was then he noticed that she had kept one hand behind her back the whole time. With a flick of his wrist, he spun her around before she could fathom his intent and the item she had tried to conceal was his.

She squealed in alarm and tried to grab it off him but he just held it out of her reach.

"My, what is this, Miss Roberts? Something nefarious perhaps?"

He held her captive with one hand whilst holding the little envelope up and with a little contortion, the contents were revealed. It was powder.

"What trickery is this?" He exclaimed, looking down at her. "Well?"

"It is... errr...!"

"I can see you are going to need a bit of persuasion, let me help you."

He pulled her over to the edge of the bed and placing the envelope on the bedside table, he drew Amelia straight down over his thighs as he sat down on the mattress.

"What are you doing?!" she gasped.

"I am going to spank you until you tell me what that powder is. I know it's something bad and I also know that within a few minutes you are going to tell me the truth."

"You can't do this!" She yelped.

He handed her a pillow. "If you don't want anyone to hear, then you may wish to use this pillow to stifle your cries, because either way you are in for a sound spanking."

Amelia couldn't believe her ears! He was going to spank her! How dare he? Could she stop him by revealing what the powder was? She pulled a face, reasoning that would only make matters worse.

She felt him lift her skirts and petticoats and then shockingly he untied her bloomers and pulled them aside, so her bare bottom was on view.

She kicked her legs out in protest but he stopped her instantly by throwing one of his long legs over hers, effectively preventing any further movement.

"You don't have to do this!" Amelia complained.

Suddenly, his hand came crashing down on both cheeks. She gasped and tried to throw her hand around to protect her bottom but he just slapped it aside.

"Do that again and I shall make this even longer!" He warned her.

Amelia's eyes widened and burying her head in the pillow, she braced herself for the next smack.

Oliver set up a steady rhythm, smacking one cheek and then the other until she could hardly breathe.

He paused, leaving his hand laying on her heated skin and asked, "So, we will try again. What is the powder?"

She raised her head from the pillow and asked, "If I tell you, will you refrain from spanking me further?"

"That all depends on what it is."

She thought hard. What could she tell him it was? Oh, lord.

"Well?"

"It was just a little prank. I didn't mean anything by it. Truly." She swallowed hard and then said in a rush, "It is just a little itching powder, that's all."

"Itching powder." She heard him utter a low laugh. "You are a wilful madam, Miss Roberts. Do tell me what I did to deserve such wrath?"

His hand on her bottom was doing funny things to her stomach. It was such an intimate thing to do and she didn't quite understand her feelings. She glanced over her shoulder to look at him and their eyes met. She pouted and said, "Well, you kept going on about my drinking tonight and it made me angry."

"So you thought you could sneak in here and ply itching powder to my clothes."

"That was my intention." She wasn't about to reveal that she had already put it on his night attire.

He looked down at her bottom and, noting the bright red hue, said, "Well, I think that is fair punishment for your wayward behaviour." And with one resounding smack, which made her gasp at the intensity, she felt him retying her bloomers, before he lowered her skirts and petticoats and allowed her to stand. She rubbed the tender skin through the fabric, pulling a face whilst doing so.

"I assume you won't do it again?" he asked.

She shook her head, her eyes settling on his. "No, I promise."

Her bottom felt as though it were on fire and she knew that sitting down tomorrow would be very difficult indeed. It would seem that trying to best Lord Berkeley wasn't an easy thing to do. Although there was still the tainted nightshirt.

Hiding the wicked smile that threatened to break out on her face, she remained trite and apologetic before leaving his room and heading to her own.

Oh, Lord Berkeley, what a sleep you will have tonight!

⁓ ❧ ⁓

At breakfast the next morning, Amelia took her seat at the table next to her mother. It had taken her a long while to get to sleep last night, not only from her throbbing hot bottom but because she couldn't stop thinking about Lord Berkeley.

Being draped over his strong muscular thighs had stirred emotions in her that she never knew existed apart from within the pages of a steamy novel. No man had ever made her feel like that. But what she was having a hard time accepting was that he had punished her. Surely she should feel the complete opposite. She should loathe him. Yet, she didn't.

Opting for the scrambled eggs and toast, she started her breakfast just as Lord Berkeley and her brother entered the room. She glanced up and was just in time to see him shoot her a look of reprove, whilst absently scratching his arm.

For a moment she wondered why he was so clearly annoyed and then she remembered the nightshirt. He must have worn it.

Oh, what beautiful revenge. She tittered into her serviette and looked away, her eyes sparkling with devilment.

That would teach him. Now all she had to do was stay out his way just in case he wanted to dish out another spanking!

A *month later...*
Amelia looked out of her bedroom window and was happy to see the sun shining. In fact, it was quite a beautiful day. The snow had disappeared over two weeks ago and now the ground was quite dry in places. It was the end of February and the early spring flowers were starting to appear from their winter slumber. Crocuses were her favourite and she could already see their vibrant colours in the flower beds and scattered around the base of the tall trees.

She quite fancied a ride this afternoon. She had been cooped up for too long due to the icy cold conditions and today was the first time in a while that she had the urge to go out.

She would head over to Cora's house and pay her a visit. They hadn't seen one another since her sister's wedding and she surmised they would have plenty to talk about. Her thoughts turned to her sister, Florence. She had come to visit only yesterday and she looked quite vibrant. Marriage suited her well and it would seem that her husband was keeping her happy. Very happy indeed!

Would she one day find such happiness? An image of Lord Berkeley came to mind, his dark eyes penetrating and foreboding. She shivered a little, remembering his hard hands smacking her bottom and imagined being married to such a man. Good lord, she would have to learn to behave if she were his wife.

She pulled a face. When and if she married, she would prefer a man far more amenable than Lord Berkeley. Someone who would see to her every whim and fancy, a man she could wrap around her little finger to do her bidding. She had a feeling that Lord Berkeley would do none of those things!

Anna came bustling in, interrupting her thoughts. "Your father has said to dress for luncheon. We have guests coming."

Amelia turned around and looked at her, "Oh? Do you know who they are?"

Anna stopped for a moment to think and then said, "The town constable and I think he mentioned the Mayor."

"Oh, I can't stand Mayor Langley. He consumes food like it's going out of fashion!"

"Hush!" Anna scolded her. "You cannot say things like that."

"I just did. Besides, it's true. It's like watching a pig eat from a trough." She sniggered and Anna couldn't help but join in.

"Oh dear me, Mistress Amelia. Desist at once, else someone overhear us and we both get into trouble!"

When Amelia's mirth subsided she thought about the dinner guests and wondered why they had both come to dinner. "Do you think there is something amiss? Did Father look concerned to you when you saw him earlier?" she queried.

Anna nodded, "In all truth, he did look quite serious." She bustled over to the large wardrobe, opened the door and started rifling through the many dresses hanging up inside. "Now, which dress would you like to wear? I would suggest the dark green or navy blue."

Very soon, Amelia was sitting in front of the vanity mirror having her long golden locks brushed until they shone. Anna then expertly wound the hair into an elegant knot at the nape of her neck, securing it with pins and combs adorned with pearls. She had opted for the dark green silk dress so Anna added a matching ribbon, tying a neat bow above the knot.

Anna smiled with satisfaction and placing her hands on Amelia's slender shoulders, she leaned close and said, "You look as pretty as a picture."

Amelia grinned and stood up, ready to go down to make an appearance. One thing her father was a stickler for, was dressing smartly in front of guests. Leaving the room, she made her way along the corridor and then down the wide sweeping staircase.

Halfway down, she stopped in her tracks, the small smile on her face quickly turning to a small O of surprise. For standing in the hallway looking directly at her was the formidable Lord Berkeley.

Oliver had just entered the large hall at Evesham along with Clarence, who had invited him to dine with them today. He had wondered if Miss Roberts would be present and was pleasantly surprised to see a vision of beauty appear on the stairs. She looked stunning. And even though he knew her precocious nature, he still felt an attraction that he couldn't deny.

He then remembered the itching powder and a small frown marred his brow. That was something he was most definitely going to admonish her for later. He wasn't about to forget what happened. His eyes darkened as he watched her descend the last steps and he noted her expression become wary.

Good, he thought. She knew she was in trouble.

Clarence had just handed over his overcoat to Simmons and, turning around, noticed his sister.

"Amelia, you look lovely, doesn't she, Lord Oliver?"

Oliver nodded his head, "Miss Roberts, I concur, you look enchanting." He saw a brief look of surprise in her eyes before she lowered her lashes, clearly unsure of how to take him. She knew she wasn't going to get away with the itching powder incident but was obviously a bit taken aback at his flattering remark.

"I didn't know you were dining with us today? I thought you were staying in Woolwich." She said, looking a little uncomfortable.

"We had a client cancel at the last minute, so I took the opportunity to invite Lord Oliver to dinner." He held his arm out to her, "Take my arm and I shall escort you in," Clarence said, grinning, "unless you would rather Lord Oliver have the honour?"

Oliver watched her eyes widen and she quickly replied, "No, no, it's fine."

Her cheeks were slightly flushed and it heartened him to see the effect he was having on her. For, in all truth, she was most definitely having the same effect on him.

Simmons obliged, by opening the dining room door and Amelia gracefully made her entrance.

Her mother and father were already seated at the long, polished table along with the two other guests.

"Ah, here are my son and daughter. And Lord Berkeley, you are most welcome!" exclaimed her father. "Please take a seat."

Simmons was instantly by their side, pulling the chairs out and making sure they were settled before heading off to the kitchens to organize the staff to begin luncheon service.

Their father introduced Oliver to Constable Atkins and Mayor Langley. Constable Atkins seemed very dour. He had a very long moustache, rather bushy eyebrows and he had seen more fat on a piece of bacon. Mayor Langley was the complete opposite. He was a jovial man with a very large stomach. So large, in fact that it was straining within the confinements of his waistcoat. He wouldn't be surprised if the buttons were to ping off during luncheon!

His attention was diverted when Simmons arrived with several staff to begin serving the first course.

Amelia accepted a glass of wine from the servant hovering nearby and took a delicate sip. She was very conscious of Lord Berkeley sitting next to her and had a feeling he would be watching how much she consumed.

Her mother broke into her thoughts, "You look rather lovely this evening," she remarked, giving Amelia's arm an affectionate pat. "That gown becomes you."

Amelia smiled, "Thank you, Mama."

As the first course of soup and bread was served, Amelia finally learned why the Mayor and Constable were there when they turned their conversation to a very serious matter.

"I say, have any of you noticed an increase in pickpockets about town lately?" asked Constable Atkins, dabbing at his moustache with a napkin.

"Indeed, I have not personally but my friend, Percy, almost had his pocket watch lifted the other day in the market," replied Clarence. "The scoundrel would have got away with it too if a constable hadn't happened by."

The Mayor nodded sagely. "It is unfortunate but not unexpected, given the hard times." He slurped a spoonful of soup before continuing, "We are, however, looking for one man in particular. A man by the name of Rufus Armstrong."

"Oh?" Mrs. Roberts said.

Constable Atkins took up the story, "He is a scoundrel by all accounts, having duped many people into parting with their money and now he has been accused of pickpocketing. It is most unfortunate."

"And this happened in Rochester?" Lord Berkeley asked. The Constable nodded.

Clarence's countenance turned grim, "Do you have a description of the man? Perhaps when we are in town next we can keep a lookout for the villain."

"Indeed we do." Constable Atkins reached inside his waistcoat and pulled out a roll of paper. He unfurled it and handed it to Clarence who held it up so both he and Oliver could see.

"I haven't seen him before." Clarence said, looking at the drawing, "He looks quite a handsome fellow but there is a mean glint in his eyes."

"Do you have reason to believe he is still in the vicinity?" Lord Berkeley asked.

"Indeed we do. It is why we are visiting each house to warn the inhabitants. Make sure to keep your doors locked and have your servants vigilant to the comings and goings of everyone in the household. Just until he's caught."

"I shall have to be extra vigilant with my purse in the coming days." Amelia heard her mother exclaim, her face full of worry.

Mr. Roberts turned to her and said, "I think, my dear, that you should stay here until this man has been caught." Amelia watched her father pat her mother's hand and waited for the eruption she knew that would follow.

"Mr. Roberts! You expect me to stay at home when you know that I always meet Mrs. Athelthorpe on Thursday afternoons!" She exclaimed indignantly. "I am not going to let some... some ne'er do well stop me from perusing the shops and boutiques in town!"

Amelia finished her soup and dabbed at her mouth delicately with her napkin, trying to hide the smirk that threatened to break out. If her father saw her amusement he would certainly reprimand her later.

"We shall discuss the matter another time." Her father said, his tone implying that the subject was closed for now. Her mother gave a disgruntled sigh, but knew that now was not the time to argue.

As the soup bowls were cleared away, the servants began bringing out the next part of the meal. Succulent roast beef, steaming vegetables fresh from their own gardens and buttery mashed potatoes.

Amelia accepted her portion of roast beef, carved thinly by Simmons, along with a generous helping of the vegetables. She glanced over to see Mayor Langley's plate piled high, it appeared to be almost treble the quantity of hers. She happened to glance over at her brother and he pushed his nose up imitating a pig.

It immediately caught her sense of humour and she started laughing. Her father looked at her sharply so she quickly picked up her napkin and turned it into a cough. "Oh, do excuse me. I think a piece of the beef went down the wrong way."

She didn't dare look at Clarence as it would just set her off again, so she tucked into her meal avoiding his gaze. She thought she heard a tut of disapproval from Lord Berkeley but chose to ignore him.

Constable Atkins was also enjoying the meal with gusto. "This beef is exquisite!" He marvelled as he cut into his portion.

"I will be certain to pass along your compliments to our cook," replied Mr. Roberts.

"It is always a pleasure to dine at Evesham Manor," Mayor Langley remarked, forking a big piece of beef and holding it aloft. "You always do offer the most wonderful hospitality."

With the meal finished and coffee to be served in the parlour, Amelia chose to go outside into the garden, craving some solitary air. She needed to walk off her dinner for her ride later that afternoon and in all truth, she wanted to avoid any confrontation with the strict Lord Berkeley.

She had a feeling he was going to reprimand her for putting itching powder in his nightshirt and she didn't fancy hanging around to find out. A man like him wouldn't let the matter slide, she was certain of that!

So, just in case he decided to follow her, she darted around the back of the house following a gravel path that led to the secluded walled garden where the hedges were kept neatly trimmed under the watchful eye of the head gardener.

With all the different sections it would be very hard to find her, very hard indeed!

Chapter Four

Amelia hurried down the garden path, hoping the high walls and leafy greenery would conceal her from view. She didn't doubt for a moment that Lord Berkeley would come looking for her. That look he had given her earlier had been enough for her to know that he hadn't forgiven her for the nightshirt.

She pulled a face, wondering if he would dare to spank her again. No, surely not! Hadn't she been punished enough?

She sat down on a stone bench and looked around. It was so peaceful and relaxing, just her and the birdsong. After a few tense minutes, she started to relax, realising that if he did arrive, then she would most certainly hear him.

She just hoped he wouldn't find her! Or did she?

She had to admit that he intrigued her. She couldn't help but respond to his masculine strength. He may be strict and foreboding but, dare she say it, it ignited a fire in her bosom that she couldn't deny.

"Ah, there you are, Miss Roberts. I have been looking for you." Amelia nearly jumped out of her skin when Lord Berkeley emerged from behind a nearby hedge.

It would seem that her secret hiding place was not so secret after all. Oh, lord.

Her hand flew to her racing heart and she said, "You frightened me! I didn't even hear you!"

Oliver frowned. "Forgive me. I didn't mean to frighten you although I do wish to talk with you." He looked at the empty place next to her, "May I?"

She would have liked to say no but it would have been far too rude, so she just nodded. He took a seat and she shuffled away from him slightly, her face set. He was still close and she could smell his heady cologne. Blinking hard, she tried to stop the desire that coursed through her.

"I am here for an apology." he said without preamble.

She sucked in a deep breath. She was right. She knew it. Men like him didn't forget a thing! Raising her chin she tried to profess innocence.

"For what?"

"Do not think me a fool, Miss Roberts."

Amelia looked away, biting her lip. Should she confess or not? In a quandary she kept quiet, thinking hard.

"I will give you a choice." He turned his head and settled his eyes on her. "You either apologise for putting itching powder in my nightshirt or I am quite happy to put you straight over my knees here and spank your defiant little behind."

Amelia gasped with a mixture of shock and desire. He shouldn't speak to her like that! She jumped up and went to move away but his hand shot out and grabbed her wrist, effectively trapping her.

"What will it be?" He asked, his voice low and commanding.

She felt a tremor run through her and her face grew warm as she looked down at his strong hand that restrained her so easily. She placed a finger on her bottom lip hesitantly and noticed that he was immediately drawn to it. Their eyes met and with no words said, he rose up and swept her into a kiss of promise under the clear blue sky.

Oliver knew what he was doing far surpassed propriety but their attraction was so strong that it couldn't be denied. Her pliable lips opened beneath his to receive his exploratory tongue, and she seemed to feel the connection as much as he.

He deepened the kiss, relishing the feel of her slender body against his own. Her hands came to rest on his chest, her fingertips pressing lightly against his shirt.

All too soon, he drew back just enough to look down into her eyes. They were soft and full of emotion. He raised his finger and traced the outline of her perfectly formed lips. "You are an enigma, Miss Roberts. You are naughty beyond reason but I find that I want to know more about you. Would you consider me as a suitor?"

"Would you want a wife so naughty?" She breathed, her eyes blazing wickedly.

"Oh indeed I would, for she would soon learn to change her ways or take the consequences." He said, a smile playing on his lips.

"Well, I will think upon it." she replied, returning his smile. "But as for learning to behave, then I cannot promise such a thing."

"I didn't think you could."

He drew her back against him and recaptured her lips. She made no objection and they were soon lost in each other's arms.

Later that afternoon, after her revelation in the garden, Amelia set out on her mare Lily for a ride across the countryside towards Cora's house. The fresh air and exercise would do her good after the emotional events of the morning.

Her mother had tried to dissuade her from travelling because of the pickpocket they'd been warned about but there had always been a risk of encountering a ne'er do well. Hence the reason she always had a little knife concealed on her person. One could never be too careful.

She urged Lily into a gentle canter as they left the manor grounds, enjoying the feel of wind in her hair beneath her riding hat. Before her stretched rolling green meadows, dotted with wildflowers in full bloom. Birds sang sweetly from the hedgerows that separated the fields. It truly was a beautiful spring day.

After about half an hour's ride, Amelia spotted the tall gates to her friend's house in the distance. She nudged Lily into a gallop, eager to unburden her heart. She was so excited to find out what her friend thought on the matter. The mare's hooves thundered across the grass.

Cora's Mother greeted her when she was led into the parlour and Amelia immediately knew by her expression that something was amiss.

"Has something happened?" Amelia asked. "Is Cora not at home?"

"She is being attended to by Doctor Hopkins."

Amelia gasped, "Is she unwell?"

"She fell off her horse yesterday. I am always telling her not to gallop so fast but she never listens to me and what happened? She was unseated and has now injured her ankle!" She wrung her hands together. "At first we thought it was just a slight sprain and that today it would have improved but this morning, she couldn't even put any weight on it."

"Oh?" Amelia said concerned, "Do you think she might have broken it?"

"Thankfully Doctor Hopkins has confirmed it is merely a sprain, although a very bad one. She will likely have to have bed rest for at least two weeks, perhaps more."

"Oh, how dreadful." Amelia commiserated. Cora loved riding and walking. Being confined for two weeks would surely drive her mad.

"Would you like a cup of tea whilst you wait?" Mrs. Spencer asked. "The doctor shouldn't be too long now."

"Oh, thank you, that would be most kind."

She was just about to ring the bell for the maid, when the doctor poked his head around the door. "May I come in?"

"Of course, Doctor Hopkins, of course. How is my daughter?"

He walked over to her, his brow a little furrowed. "I have given her some laudanum for the pain." He handed her a small brown bottle. "From tomorrow, give her one small teaspoon twice a day until the pain improves but make sure she doesn't move from that bed. As I said earlier, I think it will take at least two weeks until she is able to put any weight on it but we shall see. I will return tomorrow to see how she is."

"Oh, thank you. Would you like a beverage before you leave?"

"No, I must be on my way. But thank you for the offer."

When he had left, Mrs. Spencer led Amelia up to Cora's bedroom. She found her friend reclined against the pillows in her four-poster bed and her usual happy countenance was long gone and in its place, was a very unhappy visage indeed.

"Now my dear," her mother said, "to cheer you up, you have a visitor."

Amelia immediately sat on the side of the bed and grabbed Cora's hand. "I am so sorry to hear what happened, Cora. You must feel so frustrated."

"You don't know the half of it." She breathed. Amelia immediately sensed there was something behind her words but refrained from asking until they were alone. They had always shared secrets and she knew by her tone that she had something to reveal.

"Well, I shall leave you two to talk. I will return later to see how you are, dearest. I will get Sarah to bring some refreshments and the tea I promised you, Miss Roberts!" Her mother left the room and Cora quickly raised a hand to her forehead, closing her eyes.

Amelia stared at her, "Something has happened, hasn't it?"

Cora swallowed hard and opening her eyes, Amelia could see tears beginning to form.

"Whatever is it?"

Cora grabbed Amelia's hands and looking her directly in the eyes, asked, "If I tell you, will you promise not to tell another soul?"

"Of course!" Amelia responded, "You and I have never told on one another."

Cora looked down for a moment, "I didn't mean for things to come to this. There is a man that I thought I loved, in fact I was infatuated with him. I even kissed him." Her grip tightened on Amelia's hand. "B-But when I tried to tell him that I no longer wished to see him, he threatened to tell my parents!"

"Oh!" Amelia was shocked. She had no idea that her friend had a passion for someone, she had never ever mentioned it. She frowned, "But surely your parents will understand? He is a cad to even dare threaten such a thing. They will surely sympathise with you."

Cora shook her head and a tear slipped down her face, "It could ruin my family if revealed. He has been demanding money and threatening to tell all if I do not comply."

Amelia gasped. "The scoundrel! You can't go on like this. Perhaps we should speak to the authorities, they will know what to do."

"And have this sordid affair exposed? No, I cannot bear the shame." Cora shook her head desperately. "He is a sly one. I cannot see why I was so enamoured of him. He is handsome but he is also one of the meanest men I know."

Amelia pondered silently. "So what are you going to do?"

Cora chewed her bottom lip and then said desperately, "I was due to pay him tomorrow. Can you go and see him - give him the money?"

Amelia gasped, "Me?"

"Please, you are the only person I trust. If I don't turn up, he may arrive on the doorstep!"

Amelia sprang up from the bed and paced the room, shaking her head. "I cannot believe you are asking such a thing! This man will never stop if you keep paying him." She stopped and turned to her friend, "How long are you going to let him blackmail you like this? How long, Cora?" Her voice ended on a high note.

"*Shhhh!* Someone will hear you!" Cora hissed.

Amelia sat back down on the bed next to her. "Lord, I have been asked to do some odd things but this takes the biscuit." She nibbled her nail nervously. "Where does he live? Do I know him?"

She shook her head, "He is not from around here. I met him in town whilst he was working at the stables and he was so handsome and attentive, that I just found myself falling for him. I know I shouldn't have but he has a way about him. A charm." She looked down at the coverlet, plucking absently at it as she admitted, "I was a fool."

"So he is no gentleman of standing then?"

Cora shook her head. "He comes to Rochester every month to collect his blackmail money. I always meet him at the back of the Blackwater Tavern." She raised sad eyes to Amelia. "Please don't think badly of me, Amelia. I couldn't bear that."

Amelia patted Cora's hand. "I would never think badly of you, Cora although I do think you have behaved rather carelessly." she sighed, "So your next rendezvous with him is tomorrow, is that so?"

"Yes. I usually slip out after midnight and meet him shortly after." She paused, searching her friend's face, "Will you do it for me? Just this once? When my ankle is healed, I will be able to meet him and pay him myself."

"Oh, lord, what on earth am I getting myself into!" Amelia said, her eyes wide. But she knew she would have to do it. Her friend was so desperate and in dire need of her help. How could she turn her down?

"Very well. As it is only once I will do it for you. But you truly have to contact a policeman about this. You cannot let such a varmint control your life. Blackmail is a terrible trait and he will continue as long as you let him."

"You are a true friend and I promise to do as you advise. As soon as my ankle is healed I will be able to deal with him and think clearly. At the moment I am unable to do anything!" She spread her arms wide, looking down at her bandaged ankle.

Amelia's intention to tell her friend about her blooming love for Lord Berkeley would have to wait for another day. She wasn't in the mood for good tidings and to be honest, she was very fearful of her mission the next night. She just hoped nothing went wrong.

She stood up and brushed her skirt down, "Have you got the money in here?"

Cora pointed to the top drawer of her commode. "It's in there. Take out ten guineas."

Amelia looked at her askance. "Ten guineas! Is that how much you have to pay him?" Cora nodded. "That is an absolute disgrace! The whole thing is a disgrace!"

"Please, Amelia, just this once."

Amelia sighed and opening the drawer, took out the small pouch and counted out ten guineas. She slipped the coins in her riding habit pocket and returned to the bed. "So how will I know this man? I presume he has a name? And what does he look like?"

"He has dark brown, almost black hair, a moustache and very dark brown eyes. His name is Rufus Armstrong."

Amelia's jaw couldn't have dropped any lower if she had tried and she looked at her friend in horror! "Did you say Rufus Armstrong?"

Cora nodded.

"Oh my!" Amelia said, collapsing into a nearby chair. "What on earth have I got myself into?"

The next night

The night was dark as Amelia made her way through the shadowy alleys of Rochester's seedier districts. She pulled her cloak tighter, trying to avoid the unsavory characters lurking in doorways. How she had the nerve to do this she had no idea. She should have just gone behind her friend's back and told Constable Atkins of her discovery. But she knew she would never betray her friend's confidence.

She had walked the half an hour distance from her home as waking the stable lads to saddle her horse would have been a foolish move indeed. She usually liked walking and was no stranger to a hearty walk in the countryside but this was nothing like that.

Finally, she spotted the dim light of a tavern up ahead, its sign creaking in the breeze - The Blackwater Tavern. Taking a steadying breath, she walked past the main door and made her way around the back of the building.

Raucous laughter and slurred voices assaulted her ears coming from inside the dingy excuse for an inn and it caused her to shudder. She moved faster, wanting the ordeal to be over as quickly as possible.

Rounding the corner of the building, she could make out a small light, flickering in the corner, next to it, a lone figure stood silently waiting.

Amelia gulped and had to resist the urge to run. She clutched the bag of coins and ventured forward, hesitantly, her heart thumping so loudly she was certain he would hear.

Even in the dim light, she could see he had the look of a scoundrel. Yes, he was handsome in a ruggish kind of way. Dark unkempt hair fell over his face and his coat, although finely tailored, was worn and shabby.

As she approached, she whispered, "Are you Mr. Armstrong?"

He stepped forward and she gulped nervously, her breathing almost stopping with fear.

"Who's asking?"

He peered at her, his dark eyes glinting like black coal in the gloomy light and then he gave her a roguish smile. "Well, well, what's a fine lady like yerself doin' in a place like this?"

Amelia steeled her nerves. "I have come in place of Miss Cora Spencer."

He looked a little surprised for a second but quickly covered it, "Why ain't she 'ere 'erself?"

"She-She has injured her ankle and asked me to deliver the money. Ten guineas isn't it?"

She held out the bag of coins, her hand shaking so much she thought she would surely drop it.

He took it from her hands but in doing so, grabbed her wrist. "What are you doing?" she yelped. "Let go this instant!"

"No one knows you're 'ere do they?"

Amelia tried to wrench her wrist free but his grip was like iron. He pulled her against him and looking her in the eyes said, "What else 'ave you got on yuh?"

"N-Nothing!" She tried to pull back, "Now let me go."

"What if I don't wanna, eh?" He leaned his mouth down to hers and involuntarily she screamed.

Suddenly, she heard a whistle being blown and heavy footsteps running towards them. Rufus turned to look and found himself staring at the full beam of a gas lamp. It was the police.

"That's Rufus Armstrong!" One of them yelled. "Get him!"

Rufus pushed Amelia away so hard in his quest to escape that she stumbled backwards. Quickly righting herself she also went to run. The last thing she wanted was anyone finding her in the vicinity.

But her attempts to run were thwarted when a pair of hands wrapped around her waist and lifted her into the air. She squealed and then immediately hushed when she heard who it was.

"Don't even think of running. You have some questions to answer, madam!" It was Lord Berkeley. What on earth was he doing there?

Desperate to get away, she did the unthinkable and kicked him in the nether regions. She had no choice. As he let out a howl of pain, he still managed to reach out a hand to try and grab her ankle. He only succeeded in getting her shoe.

As fast as she could, she ran hell for leather towards the path that led to home. Even though she only had one shoe and the stones cut into her stockinged foot, she didn't stop. Not for one minute. Even when a stitch began to form in her side, she ran. Only when she reached the safe confines of Evesham Manor did she finally collapse within the grounds and sob with relief.

She had never been happier to be home.

Chapter Five

The next day

How Amelia managed to sleep the previous night, she had no idea. She awoke slowly, stretching her weary body. Lord, her limbs ached! The journey home had been horrendous. Just the thought of Lord Berkeley catching her and having to confess what she had been involved with, had driven the fear of god into her.

He would never want her for a wife after that.

She pulled her right foot out from beneath the covers and looked at the sole. It was red and sore from the stones she had trod on. Thankfully, the stockings she had worn were quite thick. She glanced over at them, noticing the holes and dirt on the one that had taken the brunt of the ground. Lord, if Anna saw that, she'd be in so much trouble.

Sliding her legs from under the covers, she reached over and quickly grabbed them, stuffing them under her pillow. Then she noticed her lone shoe. The other that had been ripped off in the scuffle with Lord Berkeley was most probably still lying on the dusty street in Rochester.

She pulled a face. She really should have just said no to Cora. Apparently for every problem there was a solution but in their case, there was just another problem. Eugh. She kicked the offending shoe under the bed, hoping she would forget about it.

Constable Atkins sat at his desk in the police station and stared at the little shoe in front of him, whilst idly twisting the ends of his rather fine moustache.

"I can't believe we nearly had the blighter." He lamented.

"He was quicker than a fox." Oliver remarked. "I wonder who the woman was with him?"

Mayor Langley picked up the shoe and held it up to the light. "It was most fortuitous that you were there Lord Berkeley. If not, we would never have this piece of evidence. It was a shame, however, that the woman managed to get away." He raised an eyebrow, "She was quite petite I am told."

"Indeed she was." Oliver shifted uncomfortably remembering how painful a blow she had dealt him. She might have been small in stature but she knew exactly where to deal a death blow! Personally, he would rather not have had such a memorable end to his evening in Rochester with Clarence.

Constable Atkins slapped his hand on the desk. "Well, we have the right shoe so there must be an owner to the left shoe. If you look here at these dark red buttons, I would say, they are rather unique and the shoe looks to be quite new and I deduce gentlemen that they belong to a lady of means."

Oliver looked over and after a brief examination, concurred the same. "Well, gentleman, you have my statement so I will bid you good day and do please let me know when you catch the man. I think we will all rest better when he is behind bars."

Amelia urged her mare Lily into a swift canter along the wooded trail. After her ordeal last night, she needed to tell Cora what had happened and if possible, get her to inform her parents. She really couldn't go on like this.

As the trees flew by, Amelia's troubled thoughts turned to Lord Berkeley. She felt terrible for causing him pain but she had had no choice. If she hadn't she could very well have been interrogated or worse still, arrested. Imagine the scandal. Her cheeks grew hot at the thought. She doubted she would ever recover from the furore that would ensue.

Arriving at Cora's house, she quickly dismounted and went inside. The doctor had already been and gone, so Amelia was shown straight up to her room.

When the door was shut and they were quite alone, Amelia recounted her tale in hushed tones. When she finished, Cora looked as white as a sheet.

"Oh my, Amelia. I never thought Rufus would do such a thing! What if the police hadn't of come along! Oh dear me. I feel terrible."

"I think there is only one solution to this and you are going to have to tell your parents."

"I can't, Amelia. Can you imagine!"

"Then inform the police. They already know about him as he has been pickpocketing. Did you know about that?"

Cora covered her face with her small hands and began to cry. "Oh dear. I have made such a mess of my life."

Amelia wrapped her arms around her, trying to give comfort but in all truth, her words were correct. She should never have got involved with such a low down varmint.

"I think, when you are recovered, we will go to see the constable together. There may be some way we can do this without your parents ever finding out."

Her words seemed to cheer Cora up and her tears started to abate. "You are such a wonderful friend. I am so glad to have you."

Amelia gave her a warm smile. "Now, dry those tears and I will read a book to you." Reaching into her small bag, she withdrew a little book and held it up for Cora to see. It was a saucy little novel that she had snaffled from Clarence's bedroom.

Her eyes widened, "Where did you get that?"

"Oh, I have my sources. Now, don't you feel better already?" She grinned and settling herself on a chair, began to read.

Something was bothering Oliver. There was something about that woman that he had got away that seemed so familiar yet he couldn't quite place her. It was her perfume. He had smelled it before. But where?

Shaking his head, he realised that maybe it was just a common scent. Lots of women used perfume so of course, he would have smelled it before.

Dismissing it from his mind, he cantered towards Evesham Manor. He needed to see Miss Roberts. He had thought of nothing but her beautiful lips since he had kissed her. She was perfection. She fit into his arms as though they were both carved from the same tree.

Entering through the gates, he cantered up the drive and gave his horse into the keeping of the stable lad.

Simmons received him into the grand hallway and informed him that Miss Roberts wasn't home. She was, however, expected later that afternoon if he wished to wait.

Oliver couldn't help but be disappointed. Whilst he stood pondering whether or not to stay or go home, he saw Anna coming down the stairs carrying a bundle of laundry. On the last step she managed to trip and would have gone flying if not for Oliver's quick actions.

He caught her just in time. The laundry fell from her hands onto the polished floor but she herself was unharmed. She righted herself with his help and thanked him profusely. "Goodness me, Lord Berkeley. I am not sure how I managed to do that!"

He smiled and started to pick up her laundry. It was then he noticed the shoe. The same shoe that was currently in the police station's evidence box.

Only this one was the left shoe, whereas the other was the right.

"May I ask where this shoe came from?"

Anna took it from him, "Oh, this is Mistress Amelia's. She somehow managed to lose the other one, so I was going to throw it away."

Oliver went quiet as his thoughts took a sinister turn. Surely not? Not his Amelia? She couldn't be involved with a nefarious brute like Rufus Armstrong?

Feeling a mixture of anger and dismay, he tried to act nonchalant so as not to raise any concern. "Do you know how she managed to lose the other one?"

"No, she's a bit of a minx, so it could be anywhere. I shall order a new pair to be made. It is no bother."

"May I take that one?"

She looked at him a bit oddly, "You want this shoe?"

He nodded and not wishing to alert anyone to any wrongdoing or get Miss Roberts into any trouble, he quickly thought of an excuse, "I know a good cobbler in Woolwich. I may be able to get him to make a matching shoe. After all, it does seem such a waste to get rid of this one when it seems to have hardly any wear."

Anna nodded in agreement and handed it to him, "You are so right, my Lord. If only everyone thought like you and weren't so frivolous!"

"Indeed." He turned to leave and then asked her, "Where did Miss Roberts go this afternoon? Perhaps I could ride out and meet her halfway."

"She is visiting Miss Spencer over at Abbeyfield. If you go down the lane and turn right, continue straight ahead and it's the first house you come across.

He thanked her and leaving the house, made his way to the stables to collect his horse. His mind was in a whirl and he knew that the wilful Miss Roberts had a lot of explaining to do!

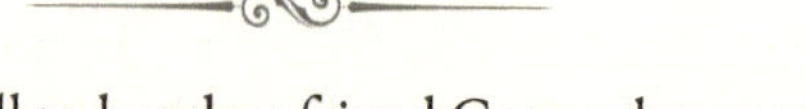

Amelia bid farewell to her dear friend Cora, who was feeling much lighter of spirit after listening to her read from the rather risqué novel and promised to return in a couple of days. Book in hand of course, she thought to herself grinning. They still had a few delicious chapters to read.

She mounted Lily and departed for home. As she rode the winding forest paths homeward, the late afternoon sun dappled the ground with gold. Birdsong filled the air as they flitted between the trees. Amelia inhaled deeply the scents of pine and earth, letting nature's calm soothe her frayed nerves.

Lily's hooves moved surely over the familiar trails and it wasn't long before they left the forest behind, entering out onto the sunlit meadows. For a moment, the sun blinded her and she held her hand up to shield her eyes.

It was then that she spotted a familiar silhouette in the distance. A tall rider atop a chestnut stallion was cantering leisurely towards her. Even from afar, she would know that dashing form anywhere. It was Lord Berkeley.

She felt her heart begin to hammer as much with excitement as trepidation. What if he had recognised her last night. She knew that the only thing she could do was to act casual, so raising her hand she waved at him.

He responded immediately and lifted a hand in greeting. Amelia nudged Lily into a gallop, closing the distance between them swiftly.

When they met, Lord Berkeley reined in his horse next to hers. "Miss Roberts, I was hoping to meet you on your return," he said with a smile but his eyes seemed a little guarded.

Her heart started to beat a little faster than usual and her hands tightened on the reins. What if he knew? Oh lord. She must remain calm otherwise he would definitely notice something amiss. One careless slip could mean the end of everything – her reputation, her family's good name, and quite possibly her future with Lord Berkeley as well. Not to mention, the trouble it would cause for Cora.

Maybe she was just reading too much into it, she thought trying to convince herself that everything was fine. After all, she had managed to escape his hold before he had a chance to see her face. And in the dark it would have been nigh on impossible to see her features. Yes, she was most definitely overthinking it all and worrying needlessly.

Raising her chin and trying to pretend that everything was fine, she shot him a smile and said, "Lord Berkeley, I had no idea you would be visiting today."

"No, I was in town so I thought I would come to see you." He dismounted and then held his hand up to her, his eyes dark and unfathomable. Her heart skipped a beat. Part of her wanted to kick Lily into a gallop and head home as quickly as possible but even if he did suspect it had been her last night, he had no proof. So she decided that her best bet was to brazen it out. She held out her hand and he helped her to the ground.

Silently, she followed him as he led his horse over to a small copse at the end of the field. Something was definitely on his mind.

Tethering their horses to a low branch, Lord Berkeley took her hand. His touch was electric. He turned her to face him, still holding her hand.

"I have a problem and I wondered if you could help me?"

"Oh, err... yes of course. What is it?"

Oliver looked at Miss Robert assessingly before continuing. "I happened to be in town last night with your brother and upon leaving, I encountered Constable Atkins."

He noted her cheeks start to flush.

"Oh, did he have any more to say about the pickpocket? What was his name... Rufus something or other."

"Rufus Armstrong."

"Oh yes, I had forgotten."

He tried to hide the frown that threatened to break on his brow. She knew damned well who he was!

Continuing, he said, "Well, in actual fact whilst talking to the Constable, a man ran up to tell him that Rufus Armstrong had been seen nearby."

He noticed her eyes widen and she drew her bottom lip in with her little teeth. "Did the Constable catch him?"

"Unfortunately, no."

"Oh, dear!" She breathed, "then the scoundrel is still on the loose. We shall all have to remain vigilant."

She was putting on such a great act that he began to doubt that she was truly involved. But he had the evidence. Well, he had three pieces of evidence to be precise: the shoe, her petite stature and another damning piece was her perfume. When he had lifted her down from her horse, the distinct fragrance had assailed his senses and he immediately recognised it from last night.

"We will indeed. But there is another problem. There happened to be a woman with him. We don't know how she is involved or why she was there but Constable Atkins would dearly like to talk to her."

"A woman?" The flush on her face deepened.

Oliver nodded, "She tried to run away and I almost caught her but she escaped my clutches. However, in the process I ripped off her shoe. It's at the police station now as evidence."

He noticed a look of alarm cross her face and she quickly tried to hide it. "What could they possibly hope to find out by keeping her shoe? It seems a silly bit of evidence to keep if you ask me."

"Not at all. In fact, I studied it in detail which is why, when I went to your house earlier, I immediately recognised the same shoe."

At that revelation she couldn't hide her gasp. Her eyes flashed with fear.

"What do you mean?"

He opened his saddle bag and withdrew the left shoe, her shoe, and held it up for her to see.

His look dark and stern, he said accusingly, "What the devil have you got yourself involved in, Miss Roberts?"

Amelia's stomach churned as anxiety set in. Oh, lord she was in so much trouble.

She quickly blurted, "It is not my shoe! I don't know what you are accusing me of but I assure you, I wasn't in town last night." It was the only thing she could think of saying.

"So you are accusing your maid of lying, because she herself told me that this shoe belongs to you."

Her breath caught in her throat. Lord, this wasn't good. She licked her lips and tried to bluster her way out of it. "My maid is a tad forgetful. Maybe she thought it was mine and...!"

He interrupted her quickly, "Do you take me for a complete fool?"

"Of course not."

"Then tell me what you were doing in town last night with that scoundrel? What is your connection to him?"

She shuffled her feet nervously, "I told you I wasn't there last night."

"So you refuse to tell me the truth?"

Amelia could clearly see his anger and tried to back away but he grabbed hold of her wrist. "You may have escaped me last night, Miss

Roberts but I am not about to let it happen again I assure you." He pulled her over towards the copse and locating a fallen log, he quickly sat down and drew her over his lap.

"What are you doing?" she gasped. Surely he wasn't going to spank her again?

"I am going to get the truth out of you the best way I know how." She felt his hands on the hem of her riding habit and then it was drawn up over her back. Oh yes, she was in doubt as to his intention.

She struggled and kicked her legs, trying to break free but it was impossible. She was no match for his strength and very soon she felt the full impact of his large hand on her bottom.

She gasped. "Aow!" and then added, "You don't have to do this! Truly!"

She felt his hand come down again on her backside, sending a burning pain straight to her nerve endings. It stung like hell. How was she going to get out of this without telling him the truth? There was too much at stake!

She yelped as another resounding smack hit her posterior. And another.

Oliver was so angry that he couldn't even think clearly. She was clearly hiding her connection to Rufus Armstrong and thought she could lie to him of all people. He cared for her and the thought of her anywhere near the nefarious villain made his blood boil.

He smacked her twice, his hand coming down in quick succession and was satisfied to hear her yelps of pain. Perhaps this would teach her a lesson.

He paused and lay his hand against her heated flesh, her bottom quivering at his touch.

"Now, tell me, my defiant Miss Roberts, that you weren't in town last night!"

She turned and looked at him over her shoulders, her eyes flashing with a mixture of petulance and consternation. He raised an eyebrow waiting for her to speak and silently daring her to continue lying.

He could see she was having a hard time deciding what to do but in the end, his efforts paid out, "I was there to pay him blackmail money." she admitted.

Of all the things she could have said, that surprised him the most. Quickly, he pulled her upright and cradled her on his lap. "Blackmail? Against who? You?"

Her lashes lowered over her eyes and he knew she was thinking about covering up for someone so he placed his hand on her chin and made her look at him. "If you are trying to protect someone, don't."

"But if I tell you the truth, I will get someone in trouble and it's not her fault."

He looked at her full lips, pouting with sadness and wanted to kiss away her fears but first he needed her to speak the whole truth. Only then could he act upon the information.

"Tell me." His voice was low, persuasive.

He listened as she finally told him the whole sorry story and when she finished, he sat in silence contemplating his next move.

"What will you do?" she asked him.

"I think we should both go to see Constable Atkins. He is a fair and honourable man."

Her eyes widened, "I did suggest the same to Cora but I am worried he will inform her parents."

"I believe he won't. In fact, I am certain of it." He couldn't resist placing a soft kiss on her lips, "Now, don't you feel better for telling me?"

She scowled, "My bottom doesn't!"

"And who is to blame for that, Miss Roberts?" he said accusingly, "you should know not to lie to me." He kissed her again and then said, "remember this and always tell me the truth."

With smouldering dark eyes he claimed her lips for his own, leaving her in no doubt how he felt about her.

Chapter Six

The next day, Amelia rode out to visit her friend Cora once more. She couldn't say it was a comfortable ride because of her spanking yesterday. Her backside was still tender from Lord Berkeley's discipline.

But she had no choice. She needed to urgently tell Cora about what had happened between her and Lord Berkeley. He had told her that Constable Atkins would need a statement from Cora and because she was bedridden, it would have to take place at her house. Something she knew Cora was going to oppose with much vociferation.

So, she had asked Lord Berkeley to let her speak with Cora first to see if there was a way of accomplishing it without her parents at home.

As she dismounted, she spotted another horse in the stable - a fine chestnut mare that could only belong to one person.

Entering the house, her suspicions were confirmed. Seated with Cora in the bedroom having cakes and tea was the beautiful Lady Caroline Egerton, daughter of a wealthy earl. Amelia's heart sank at the sight of her. If there was one person that rubbed her up the wrong way, it was Lady Caroline! They were about the same age and had disliked each other at first sight.

She may be beautiful but she was narcissistic to the core and they had often had verbal altercations. They tolerated one another for politeness's sake but there was an obvious mutual dislike.

"Amelia, how lovely to see you." Cora said, her face lighting up. "I thought you weren't coming until tomorrow?"

"I wasn't but I changed my mind." She wouldn't mention why she was really there a day early. Not in front of Lady Caroline. She would wait until the arrogant woman had left first.

She turned and reluctantly acknowledged the woman's presence, "Good afternoon, Lady Caroline."

Lady Caroline looked at her cooly and responded with a dismissive nod, before taking a sip of her tea. Amelia curled her lip. Horrid woman.

An undercurrent of tension filled the room and Cora attempted to lighten the mood, "Mama sent up some cakes and tea, Amelia and your timing is perfect. Please help yourself."

Amelia sat down on a chair and started making herself a cup of tea.

Lady Caroline turned her attention back to Cora. "As I was saying, my dear, Lord Pembley simply dotes on me. It is only a matter of time before he declares himself, I am sure of it."

Amelia bit her tongue to hold back a retort. Poor man was going to be in for a life of torment if he truly did declare himself. Imagine being married to that harpy. She knew Lord Pembley and he was a weak individual but extremely wealthy so maybe that was the attraction.

She hid a smile and sipped on her tea as the two talked about the 'dashing' Lord Pembley. He wasn't dashing at all, in fact he was quite plain, verging on ugly. Nothing at all like her handsome beau. Her eyes grew soft when she thought of him.

"Miss Roberts, what are you thinking about that makes you smile so?" Lady Caroline said, her eyes sharp and intuitive.

"Oh, nothing you would be interested in." She neatly steered the conversation back to her. "Will you have a summer wedding?"

She noted Lady Caroline flush and realised that perhaps she was over zealous about Lord Pembley's affection for her. It sounded more like wishful thinking. Perhaps, even the dull Lord Pembley could see through her!

Raising her face arrogantly, Lady Caroline responded, "Well, we haven't discussed that as yet but I am certain we shall, very soon." Then she looked down at Amelia's dress and said nastily, "I must say, your gown is quite... interesting. Do tell, did you maid choose that particular shade?"

Amelia's eyes narrowed. "What do you mean?"

She gave a delicate laugh, "Well, it is rather dull."

"I beg your pardon?" Amelia's riding habit was a beautiful shade of green, edged with black braiding and it certainly wasn't dull!

Lady Caroline shrugged, "I am just expressing my opinion." She looked her up and down, "It suits *you* I suppose."

Amelia got her meaning straight away and felt her temper begin to surface. How dare she? Rude harlot. Trying her best to keep her voice light and sweet she said, "I chose this colour myself and it is far from dull." She eyed Lady Caroline's outfit, "It is a pity you think so but then I find your taste in fashion a little too vibrant, quite old-fashioned. One could say almost as outdated as your manners."

She was satisfied to see Lady Caroline's eyes widen in shock. "Well there is no need to be so rude! But then I suppose I shouldn't expect anything less from someone like you."

"Oh? What is that supposed to mean?"

Cora looked from one to the other and quickly said, "Now, now you two. Please. There is no need for such animosity. You are here to visit me, are you not?"

Amelia gave one last glare at Lady Caroline before turning to her friend, "How right you are, Cora. Maybe I should return later, when you are alone. I suddenly feel the need for some air."

Lady Caroline stood up. "Oh, don't mind me. I must be going. Mother has arranged a small dinner gathering tonight so I have to cut my visit short anyway." and pointedly looking at Amelia, added, "And I concur, the air is a little stale in here."

Amelia raised an eyebrow and refrained from saying anything, knowing that if she did, things could escalate pretty quickly. And that truly wouldn't be nice for Cora to behold. So biting her tongue, she waited for the odious witch to leave.

A few moments later, she was gone and Amelia sagged down in her chair. "Good lord, Cora. How can you stand that woman?"

"I didn't have much choice. Mama thinks she marvellous so showed her up here without asking." she flung her arms wide and exclaimed, "What could I say?"

"Get lost?" Amelia giggled.

Cora immediately started laughing. Now this was more like it. Back to their usual selves. It was amazing how one person could influence the whole atmosphere. Like dark clouds appearing on a sunny day.

Amelia finished her cup of tea before changing the subject. She knew what she had to tell Cora was going to change her mood instantly but it had to be discussed. She sat on the bed next to her and held her hand. "I have to discuss Rufus Armstrong with you."

Cora sat forward, "Have they found him?"

"Not yet but Lord Berkeley found out that it was me in town that night and made me confess the whole story to him. I am truly sorry, Cora but I had no choice." His large hands on her backside had seen to that.

Cora gasped, "Oh my!"

Amelia squeezed her hand, "Don't worry, he has offered to help us by speaking with Constable Atkins and he will request that your parents are not informed."

"They won't find out about my liaison with Rufus? What about your involvement?"

Amelia shook her head, "No, although I paid him the blackmail money last night, only us three know of my involvement so it will go no further." She patted her hand. "And the good thing is, that the police will know the date of your next rendez-vous with Rufus Armstrong and can lie in wait for him."

"And this whole sorry saga can be over with." Cora gave a sigh and leaned back against her pillows.

"The only problem we have is how to get your parents away from the house so that Constable Atkins can come to see you without their knowledge."

"Why does he need to see me?"

"He needs a statement from you. You know what these authorities are like. They need to talk to you directly, write it down in their little book. That sort of thing." She shrugged her slender shoulders. "So is there a time he can come?"

Cora chewed her lip, thinking hard. "At the moment Papa is up in London and not due back until the weekend. But Mama is going to see Aunt Violet in Chatham on Friday afternoon."

"What time will she be gone?"

"She sometimes dithers a bit gettin away so say three o'clock to be on the safe side. She won't be back until after six." She shot her a worried look. "What about the servants though? They are bound to tell my parents that the Constable was here?"

"Just tell them that you thought you spotted Rufus from the window or something? That should work, shouldn't it?"

"Mama will have a fit of the vapours if she thinks he's that close to the house but I can't think of anything else feasible."

"Well that's that then. I will arrange for them to call upon you Friday afternoon."

"The sooner this is over the better."

"Now then, I think we need something to lighten the mood and I just so happen to have my special book with me, so if you care to hear a little, my dear friend, I am ready to read!"

Cora shot her a wicked smile. "I am always ready for a little risqué reading!"

Amelia duly opened the book and before long, her soft lilting voice was filling the bedroom, to a very eager audience.

Lady Caroline stepped back from Cora's bedroom door where she had been eavesdropping and placed a hand over her mouth. She had heard the tail end of their conversation but that was enough. She was shocked but at the same time elated at discovering such noteworthy information.

She had only come back upstairs to retrieve the gloves she had left on the table but after overhearing such an exciting conversation, her gloves could stay exactly where they were.

So, both of those wicked girls were involved with the notorious pick-pocket Rufus Armstrong. A man the authorities were so eager to catch. Oh, my!

And oh, what good fortune!

With malicious intent, she left the house, her mind scheming on how best to use the information for her own gain.

Lord Berkeley called upon Amelia in the afternoon and she immediately led him outside to the walled gardens, where they could talk in private away from prying eyes.

He took a seat on a stone bench and she settled herself beside him. Quietly, she recounted her conversation with Cora.

When she finished, he nodded and gave a satisfied smile. "Then I shall ride into town to inform Constable Atkins this evening. We shall have that varmint behind bars before he can claim even a farthing more from Miss Spencer or indeed pick another pocket."

"What an awful man. I wish I had never set eyes on him." She shuddered and Lord Berkeley reached for her hand, softly rubbing his thumb over her sensitive skin.

"I think, after this experience, you will never get involved in anything like this again, will you?"

Amelia shook her head. "Never!"

"And you know what will happen if I find out?" He looked at her meaningfully.

Amelia's face flushed and she looked at him, "I think I know by now."

He raised her hand and kissed her knuckles, sending shivers of excitement rippling through her slender body. He was so handsome and now she knew he was someone she could rely on as well. Her love for him seared her heart.

"Do I have your permission to ask your parents if I can court you?" He asked.

"Yes," she said without hesitation, "I would like that but I have one question."

He raised an eyebrow, waiting for her to continue.

"Will you still spank me when we are married? I mean, as your wife, shouldn't you show me respect and affection, not turn me over your knee at will." On her last word, her bottom lip pouted.

He gave a low laugh, and raising her chin to his, said, "Whether you are my wife or not, if you misbehave I will see to it that you are chastised and if that means putting your naughty bottom over my lap, then I will." He placed a kiss on her pouting lips and then pulled away again. "So I warn you, my wilful little miss, that now is the time to reject me if you have any misgivings. I will have no regrets in our marriage."

Amelia eyed him carefully. He had already captured her heart so there was no doubt that she wanted him for a husband but could she learn to behave enough to stop any future spankings? She did have a penchant for getting into trouble. But then she did find the experience quite exciting. She wasn't sure why, but when he spanked her, it felt very erotic.

"I can see you are in a quandary." He said gently, "I will make you a fine husband. I have a large home, servants to see to your needs and ample income. I will worship you and see to your every need but I will, if the occasion arrives and I think you warrant it, give you a sound spanking if you put yourself in danger."

He spoke with such sincerity that Amelia just knew he meant it. And in that moment, came to her decision.

"Very well, Lord Berkeley, I accept your proposal of courtship."

Smiling broadly he lifted her up in his arms and span around. "Lord Berkeley, put me down! I shall get quite dizzy."

Reluctantly he placed her feet on the floor and pulled her straight against his strong form. His lips immediately claimed hers and she opened to him like a flower in the first rays of sun, knowing that in his arms was where she belonged.

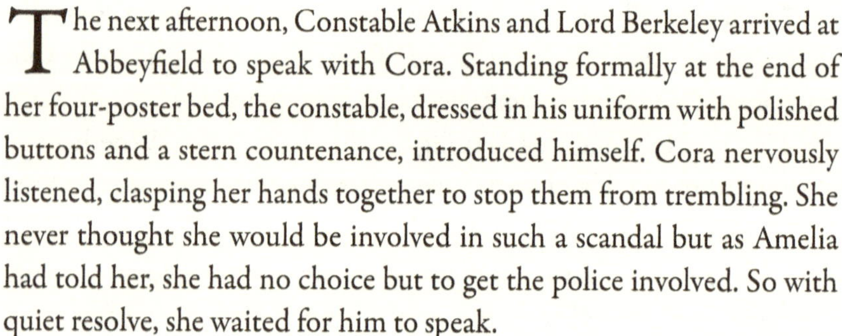

The next afternoon, Constable Atkins and Lord Berkeley arrived at Abbeyfield to speak with Cora. Standing formally at the end of her four-poster bed, the constable, dressed in his uniform with polished buttons and a stern countenance, introduced himself. Cora nervously listened, clasping her hands together to stop them from trembling. She never thought she would be involved in such a scandal but as Amelia had told her, she had no choice but to get the police involved. So with quiet resolve, she waited for him to speak.

He held out a small black book and with his pencil poised, he said, "So, Miss Spencer, I understand that you are facing a distressing situation regarding a certain gentleman by the name of Mr. Rufus Armstrong? Is that correct?"

"Yes, and I would request that what I have to tell you will go no further."

"Of course, I quite understand. When we catch the villain, we have enough evidence to convict him without your testimony. There are several witnesses who can identify him for his recent crimes, including pick-pocketing and thieving from two stores to my knowledge. There could even be more." He softened his voice a little. "I sympathise about your situation, I truly do and with your help we can catch him."

"Very well. It is just that I would rather my parents were left uninformed."

The constable leans forward slightly, exuding an air of empathy and concern. "Miss Spencer, please know that you have my full support." He motioned to a nearby chair, "May I sit down?"

"Oh of course and you too Lord Berkeley."

"I won't if you don't mind." Oliver responded. He walked over to the window and looked out across the grounds. Amelia had already recounted the whole sorry tale and he had no desire to hear it again.

He half-listened to the conversation between Miss Spencer and the constable whilst thinking about Amelia. She should never have got involved with any of this. He understood it was her friend but the kindest thing to do would have been to go straight to the police station, despite any protests from Cora.

Hopefully his actions had made her see sense. He thought about her pretty little bottom and felt a stirring in his loins. Shifting uncomfortably he tried to think of something else but it was damned hard.

He couldn't wait for her to be his. He intended to visit her parents the next day to ask their permission. He couldn't see that they would have any objection, but one never knew. Not that it would stop him.

Hearing the chair scrape back, he glanced over to see the constable rise from his chair, so he walked over to join him.

Constable Atkins closed his book and put it in his pocket along with the pencil, all the while nodding attentively, his expression one of focused concern.

"I appreciate your honesty, Miss Spencer and you can rest assured that we will do our utmost to catch him. Now we have a time and place, it will give us the advantage. He will rue the day indeed that he came to Rochester."

Cora shot him a nervous smile, "I only hope that this matter can be resolved swiftly and discreetly."

"You have my word."

With a firm nod and a genuine sense of determination, the constable turned to go. Oliver bid Cora good day and accompanied him down the stairs.

When they stepped outside onto the gravel drive, Oliver turned to Constable Atkins and asked, "Do you have enough men for the job? Mr Roberts and I could call upon others to come and help you on the night. I want this scoundrel caught."

"No, no. I will call upon the police force in Chatham as well. Catching this man is a priority. He will not escape me again."

Hearing the conviction in his voice, Oliver knew that by hook or by crook, Rufus Armstrong's days were numbered.

Chapter Seven

The next day Oliver arrived at Evesham Manor, impeccably dressed in a tailored suit and carrying a bouquet of flowers for Amelia for today he intended to speak with her parents about courting their daughter.

Amelia greeted him in the hall, her eyes lightning up at the sight of him. The desire to sweep her into his arms and kiss her senseless was overpowering but Simmons was hovering nearby so he had to make do with a simple kiss on her hand. She accepted the flowers and sniffed their heady aroma. "Oh, they are so beautiful, Lord Berkeley!"

"Not as beautiful as you, Miss Roberts." And he meant it. She looked stunning in her pale blue gown and matching ribbon in her hair. For a moment he found himself mesmerized and then remembered the reason he was there. "Are your parents at home, Miss Roberts?"

Her face flushed with excitement, knowing why he was there and she nodded, "They are in the parlour." Turning to Simmons she said, "Can you please ask my parents if they will receive Lord Berkeley?"

Oliver added, "Can you tell them it is a matter of great importance."

Simmons disappeared and Oliver took the moment to embrace Amelia and kiss her soundly. She didn't object one bit, he noted, revelling in the feel of her soft lips against his. Hearing footsteps he immediately released her, stepping back a polite distance.

Simmons inclined his head and in his usual serious manner said, "They will see you now, m'lord. If you would follow me."

With a quick look at Amelia, he left her in the hallway and followed Simmons.

Mr. and Mrs. Roberts were sitting by the fire, enjoying an after-dinner brandy. Upon being ushered into the parlour, he greeted them with a polite bow and a warm smile.

"Good afternoon, Mr. and Mrs. Roberts."

"Lord Berkeley, you are most welcome." Mrs. Roberts said, smiling.

Mr. Roberts nodded in welcome and eyed him carefully. He was known to be a strict man but fair. So Oliver came straight to the point, "I have sought this opportunity to speak with you regarding your daughter, Amelia. She has captured my affection and admiration, and if you'll permit it, I wish to formally court her."

He paused, allowing his words to sink in, whilst looking from one to the other. Mrs. Roberts smiled at her husband but Mr. Roberts merely raised an eyebrow, so Oliver added, "I assure you that my intentions are honorable, and I am committed to treating her with the utmost respect, care, and devotion. I have a large house, several servants and as you may be aware, an ample income."

Mr. Roberts studied Oliver thoughtfully. "Amelia is very dear to us. What are your intentions, should she accept your suit?"

Oliver replied truthfully, "To offer her my devotion, respect, and protection for as long as she will have me. I would cherish and care for her as my wife, should she consent to marry me."

The parents exchanged a look, then Mr. Roberts spoke. "Then you have our blessing to speak to Amelia and I speak on behalf of both of us, we wish you every happiness."

Oliver beamed, grateful and relieved for their approval to court the little minx he hoped to someday call his bride.

Amelia was on tenterhooks. She paced the hallway, waiting for Lord Berkeley to reappear and hoping with her whole being that her parents gave their permission. There was no reason why they shouldn't.

She heard the parlour door open and looked over, her heart in her mouth. One look at Lord Berkeley's countenance told her all she needed to know and her cheeks flushed pink with delight.

Rushing over to him, she asked, "They gave their blessing?"

He nodded, unable to contain his own joy. "So, my beautiful wilful Miss Roberts, will you accept my courtship?"

Amelia clasped her hands together and her eyes shining, said, "I will gladly accept, Lord Berkeley or shall I call you Oliver now?" Placing her small hand in his, she eyed him coyly, "Shall we take a walk in the gardens?"

She wanted privacy and was desperate for him to take her in his arms again.

He knew her meaning instantly and he led the way out of the front doors, down the steps to the secluded walled gardens. When they were truly alone, she was given what her heart desired when he swept her into his embrace, his powerful arms holding her against his broad chest.

She closed her eyes, breathing in his scent – a heady, masculine scent. She looked up to say something but her words were lost as his lips covered her own.

His lips ground into hers, firm and demanding, and she found her body naturally responding to his virile masculinity. He drew her even closer and buried within his powerful arms, she felt secure.

She sighed a little as he broke away, her eyes remaining closed. His kiss was so exciting, making every nerve ending tingle with anticipation. She could let him kiss her all day and soon she would be able to. When she became Lady Berkeley. When her eyelids fluttered open, he was staring at her with eyes as dark as night.

He placed a finger and thumb on her chin. "You and I are made for one another, Amelia, we make a fine couple. And now I can announce it to everyone."

"I wonder what Clarence will think of his boss marrying his sister?" She giggled.

"Hopefully he won't have any objection. Now let me kiss you again and after, I shall tell you how our meeting went with Miss Spencer."

Amelia was only too happy to fall back into his arms. What a wonderful feeling it was, when love and family approved their blossoming romance.

T*wo weeks later*

Amelia awoke with the dawn, stretching her slender legs beneath the covers and raising her hands above her head. Rolling onto her side, she sighed miserably and could hardly be bothered to get up, having slept very little last night.

She had dreamed again of Oliver's smile, his touch, and found herself longing for his presence for she had not seen him for two whole weeks. It felt like a lifetime.

He had, however, had the foresight to send her flowers every day. She pouted. That was all very well but it didn't replace one of his breathtaking kisses.

But it couldn't be helped. He and Clarence had a big legal case to deal with and had decided to take lodgings in Woolwich until it was over. She just hoped it wouldn't be much longer.

As she made her way downstairs for breakfast, Amelia's listless steps betrayed her lovesick heart. She took her seat but found she had no appetite, pushing her food idly around the plate.

Her mother noticed Amelia's melancholy demeanor. "Amelia dearest, are you unwell? You seem troubled this morning."

Amelia sighed, contemplating whether to share the reason for her sorrow. "I find myself missing Lord Berkeley dreadfully. It has been too long since I last saw him."

Her mother smiled knowingly. "Don't worry, he will be back before you know it. You know he loves you and true affection withstands any test of time or distance. Besides, he may be back in time for the spring ball."

Amelia's melancholy started to disappear and she sat up in her chair. "A spring ball?"

Her mother nodded and smiling handed her a small card. "The invitation came this morning."

Amelia scanned the card. It was the announcement of a Spring Ball to be held in the Rochester Assembly Rooms. "Oh, it's this Saturday! How exciting!"

"I thought that might cheer you up, dearest. And like I said, Lord Berkeley and your brother will likely find the time to attend. Now, why don't you go and pen a letter to Lord Berkeley inviting him to come." She reached for a piece of toast and began to butter it liberally. "They can always travel back to Woolwich the next day. I am certain one day will not harm their legal case."

She looked up just in time to see the swish of Amelia's skirts as she disappeared out of the dining room.

"Well, I gather the letter will be written sooner rather than later!" She bit into her toast, happy in the knowledge that her daughter was no longer sad.

⁓ ❧ ⁓

The evening of the ball

As the horse-drawn carriage slowly came to a stop in front of the grand Assembly Rooms, Amelia could hardly contain her excitement. Not only had she found out that her sister, Florence would be in attendance but also Oliver had sent a message to say that both he and Clarence would be coming.

What a night it was going to be!

The footman swiftly descended from his perch and opened the carriage door. Her mother stepped out first and then Amelia delicately extended her hand to grasp the footman's gloved hand for support.

She emerged from the carriage, her royal blue gown billowing softly around her in a cloud of silk and satin. The gas lamps adorning the entrance cast a warm glow, illuminating the many carriages lining the street. Her eyes sparkling with a mixture of excitement and nervousness, she waited for her father to exit the carriage and join them.

As they ascended the grand staircase leading to the entrance of the Assembly Rooms, Amelia scanned the crowd, searching for familiar faces. She soon spotted Florence and raised her hand in greeting.

Florence weaved her way through the throng of people and greeted her parents and Amelia. "It is so busy. I think after the long winter, people are desperate for some fun."

"You look very well, my dear." Her mother said.

Amelia agreed, "Marriage suits you, it would seem." She grinned and added, "I too have a suitor now. Lord Oliver Berkeley. I hope to introduce you to him tonight. He and Clarence should be arriving together so you won't be able to miss him. Besides, he is devilishly handsome!"

Florence grinned. "Oh, Amelia. I am so happy for you. What lovely news."

"Where is Albert?" her mother asked, looking around.

"He has gone to claim a table for us. There are so many people I do wonder if he will succeed."

Her face took on a worried frown and Amelia patted her arm. "Don't fret, Florence. I intend to do lots of dancing tonight, so I won't need one. As long as we find seating for Mama and Papa then all will be fine."

They made their way into the main foyer and Albert walked over to join them. "Welcome one and all," He grinned, "You will be delighted to hear I have procured a table. If you follow me!"

Florence gave a sigh of relief, "Thank goodness."

They walked past the ballroom, the sound of lively music and the swirling of dancers filling the air. Amelia glanced into the room and her heart fluttered with a mix of excitement and apprehension. She couldn't wait to join them.

Moving onwards, they entered another large room filled with small tables and chairs, all decorated prettily with linen tablecloths and vases filled with glorious flowers. To the sides were positioned more comfortable seating, for those that wished to lounge.

Suddenly, Amelia's eyes narrowed. Was that who she thought it was? Oh no, it was indeed. Lady Caroline was here. Eugh. That was all she needed! Thankfully she was on the far side of the room, so Amelia turned her head and pretended she hadn't seen her. The least she spoke to the spoiled woman, the better.

It wasn't long before Lord Oliver and Clarence arrived. They joined them at their table much to Amelia's delight. She feasted on his handsome visage. After nearly three whole weeks apart she intended to make up for lost time.

Although it was only early evening, the ball was in full swing at the Assembly Rooms, with men and women mingling in the ballroom and gardens. Lady Margaret Fotherington leaned in conspiratorially to her friend Lady Caroline, "Have you met the new gentleman, Lord Oliver Berkeley?"

Lady Caroline's eyes lit up. "I happened to see him earlier in the hall when he was introduced. His handsome good looks almost made my breath stop. Do you know where he hails from - I have never seen him before?"

"He is from nearby Chatham. His house is very grand and they say he has quite a fortune," replied Lady Margaret. "He would be quite the catch."

"Don't let your husband overhear you, Lady Margaret. I fear you would be in serious trouble!"

"Oh dear me, no. Thankfully he is outside talking with his friends." she said in hushed tones. "But what about you, Lady Caroline? I know you are courting Lord Pembley but maybe a little dalliance with a handsome man might lift your spirits."

Lady Caroline looked at her sharply, "Whatever do you mean? What is wrong with my spirit?"

Lady Margaret immediately paled, "Oh, I meant no malice. I merely observed that of late, you seem a little melancholy... I mean, nothing alarming but..."

Lady Caroline cut her short and her lips pursing she snapped, "I get your point! I suppose I have been a bit down recently but in all truth, I am unsure whether or not to marry Lord Pembley." She raised her fan and wafted it over her face. "I mean, he is such a dullard. I can say anything to him and he never so much as raises his voice."

"Isn't that a good thing? My husband never stops moaning. In fact, sometimes I confess that I make a point of keeping secrets just so he doesn't have another chance to winge."

Lady Caroline couldn't help but laugh and soon Lady Margaret was joining in, seeing the funny side of her marriage.

"From what I have learned, Lord Berkeley is well-read and well-travelled," Lady Margaret continued, "and more to the point, quite single! You simply must meet him before some other woman tries to ensnare him first. Shall we find him, so I can make the introductions?"

"Very well. I have no objection." Lady Caroline said imperiously.

The two women set off in search of Lord Berkeley, eager to put themselves in the path of this promising new prospect.

Oliver was engaged in a lively conversation with Clarence at the side of the dance floor when a rather shrill voice cut through. "Good evening, Lord Berkeley."

He turned to find Lady Margaret bearing down upon him. He had been introduced to her earlier and found her false smiles and cloying familiarity a little overbearing. "Lady Margaret," he said politely, though inwardly cringing.

"I wish to introduce you to someone." She drew him away from Clarence and waved her hand towards a woman standing nearby who was silently staring at him. "This is Lady Caroline Egerton."

Lady Margaret waited expectantly for him to greet her friend, her eyes full of meaning. Oliver knew immediately she was trying to be a matchmaker.

As soon as he clapped eyes on Lady Caroline, he knew she was someone devious. Maybe it was her superior regard of him or the sharpness he could see in her eyes. Maybe it was just intuition but he was never usually wrong.

He greeted her politely but coolly, "Good evening, Lady Caroline. Pleased to make your acquaintance."

Which was a lie but he was ever the gentleman.

"Good evening, Lord Berkeley. You are new to the area but I have already heard so much about you. I wonder, would you care to join us for a drink at our table this evening?"

"Oh, how very hospitable of you but I am afraid the little time I have this evening will be spent with family and friends. Now if you will excuse me."

But Lady Caroline was not used to being rejected and laying her hand on his arm, she looked up at him coyly. "Surely, they will afford you the time to have just one drink with us?"

He sighed inwardly. It seemed Lady Caroline was determined to make herself a nuisance.

"Forgive me, but I will be spending time with my fiancée. Now, if you will excuse me."

He nodded his head politely and quickly turned around to walk away. He hoped fervently their paths wouldn't cross again this evening. What an obnoxious, overbearing woman!

Lady Caroline was no fool and she knew a rebuff when she saw it. How dare he? And to say he had a fiancée. She rounded on her friend, Lady Margaret. "Pray tell, why did you not tell me he had a fiancée?"

Lady Margaret paled a little and started fiddling nervously with her necklace. "Truly I had no idea. It must be a recent event because I presumed him to be unattached."

"That meeting was extremely embarrassing," Lady Caroline hissed. "And I blame you entirely!"

"Hush now, my dear, people will notice." Her friend's eyes were darting around to see if Lady Caroline's raised voice was attracting any unwanted attention. Thankfully, everyone was so involved in the evening and atmosphere, that her high voice went unnoticed.

"Who is this fiancée? She must be someone noteworthy that he would choose her over me!" Lady Caroline tried to peer in the direction he had gone but there were too many people in the way. She tapped Lady Margaret with her fan. "You must find out who she is! I wish to know!"

"Is it that important?"

Lady Caroline rounded on her once more, her eyes mean and angry. "Of course it is! I must know my enemy to defeat them." She tutted loudly and spread her fan out, fanning her face rapidly. "Do I have to explain everything, Lady Margaret?"

Muttering under her breath, Lady Margaret disappeared into the crowd. If there was one thing she had learned over the years about her friend, it was that compliance was far easier than enduring her friend's fury.

Chapter Eight

Amelia had already had several dances with Oliver and each had been delightful. He was most definitely as good a dancer as she was. Whether it was the slow waltz or the energetic cotillion, he was perfectly timed and didn't tread on her feet once. A minor miracle compared to some of her previous dancers.

Slightly breathless, they made their way back to the table and sat down. Her mother smiled and poured them both a glass of champagne. "I think you two deserve this."

"Oh, that was fun." Amelia said. "I do love to dance."

"And you are extremely good at it, my dear." Oliver said, smiling.

Seated beside him, Mr. Roberts managed to capture Oliver's attention, initiating a conversation that revolved around the pressing matters of the day.

So Amelia, finding herself disinterested in the topic at hand, sat quietly observing the people in the large room. She could see no sign of her sister, so she said to her mother, "Where are Florence and Albert? Are they still dancing?"

"They went to get some fresh air outside." Her mother leaned close to Amelia and said, "I think she may be with child although she has not told me so as yet. But all the signs are there."

Amelia clapped a hand to her mouth. "Oh my!"

Her mother patted her hand. "Don't say anything until she tells you. She may not have realised yet."

"Of course, Mama. But how exciting!"

Picking up her glass of champagne, she sipped some of the delicious beverage and then realised she was quite hungry. Glancing around, she could see some empty plates on the tables and asked her mother where the food table was.

"Go through the main hall and there's a room at the back. There is a wonderful spread." She looked at her husband and Oliver. "Best not interrupt them. Just bring a selection back for Lord Berkeley. I am certain he will appreciate whatever you choose."

Amelia left the table and went in search of the food. It wasn't long before she located the buffet tables. Everything looked so delicious. At the centre were glistening hams and whole roasted fowls, their skin crisp and golden. A platter of steaks, baskets with fresh bread rolls and an array of salads.

At the other end were sweet pastries filled with cream and glazed fruits. It was all so sumptuous she didn't know what to choose.

"Oh, I wasn't expecting you to be here." A sly voice said nearby. She turned around to find Lady Caroline staring at her with a look of disdain. She was accompanied by Lady Margaret who was looking a bit uncomfortable.

Amelia raised an eyebrow. "And why shouldn't I be here?"

"It is amazing who they let in nowadays." Lady Caroline drawled.

Amelia narrowed her eyes angrily. What was her problem? Perhaps her good nature irritated her inner demons? She was, after all, a horrendous woman.

Not wishing to spoil her evening, she turned her back and picked up a plate, ready to choose some of the delectable food for her and Oliver.

"Miss Roberts, I hope you don't mind me asking but I saw you earlier talking with Lord Berkeley." Lady Margaret remarked, "Could I ask you something?"

Amelia turned to her. "Of course."

"We have heard that he is engaged. Do you know whom to?"

Oh, so that was what was bothering Lady Caroline. She fancied Lord Berkeley for herself. Smiling sweetly and trying to hide the huge satisfaction she got from her reply, she informed Lady Margaret that she, herself, was his fiancée.

"He is engaged to you!" Lady Caroline exclaimed, looking Amelia up and down as though she were an object in a display cabinet.

Amelia immediately bristled at her tone, "And what do you mean by that remark?"

Lady Caroline's laughter had an edge. "Well, you may have seen him before I did, but I can assure you if given the choice, he would choose me over you."

"I highly doubt that!" Amelia snapped, "what a ridiculous thing to say!"

Lady Caroline's eyes flashed with anger, "Your engagement is not yet set in stone. A man of Lord Berkeley's status requires a wife of equal standing - not a common girl playing at nobility."

Heat rose in Amelia's cheeks. "How dare you call me common! And just so you know I will not let you sabotage my happiness. Lord Berkeley chose me - his affection is clear, so you would do well to find your own fiancé elsewhere."

"We will see about that," Caroline sniffed. Her eyes glinted with challenge. "The night is young and one never knows what might happen." With that, she sauntered off, pulling Lady Margaret along with her and leaving Amelia trembling with anger, wondering what the conniving bitch had planned.

When Amelia returned to the table, Oliver noted she looked a little troubled. She placed a plate of food down on the table and sighed.

"Why the sigh, my love?" He asked, taking her hand and stroking the soft skin.

"I have just had the misfortune of speaking with Lady Caroline. She seems to believe that I don't deserve a fiancé like you. In fact, she thinks that you have chosen a woman below you in standing."

"She said that? What a detestable woman. I was introduced to her earlier and disliked her on sight." He knew she was trouble the moment he set eyes on her and now it was confirmed.

"She and I have never seen eye to eye. Let us speak no more of her. I will not have her ruin my evening." She showed him the plate of food. "I chose a variety of foods, so hopefully there is something here to suit your palate."

His eyes lit up and he reached for a piece of sliced ham. "I confess to being quite famished!"

"Me too." Amelia grinned.

Before long they had polished off the food and only an empty plate remained. Amelia grinned and standing up, declared that she was going back to the food table and would bring back some of the sweet pastries she had seen earlier.

"Don't be too long, else I have to come and find you." He said, "And try to stay away from Lady Caroline if you can."

When she had left he thought about what she had said. He wouldn't put it past Amelia to exact some kind of revenge on Lady Caroline. It wasn't in her nature to let things like that pass by without some sort of retaliation.

Thinking hard, he decided to follow her and keep an eye on her.

Amelia had just finished putting some pastries on her plate when Lady Margaret appeared.

"Oh, Miss Roberts. I just came to fetch Lady Caroline and I some refreshments. She quite fancies a glass of punch, so I said I would fetch one for her."

Amelia's ears pricked up. "Oh, I can get that for you. Are you having a glass as well?"

"Oh, how kind. I don't like punch, just a glass of wine for me. I am sorry for Lady Caroline's rather unfortunate vent earlier. I am sure she didn't mean it."

Oh, she meant it alright, thought Amelia. But Amelia had a cunning plan to exact revenge on the mean woman but first she had to distract Lady Margaret. "Oh, please, don't mention it. I take what she says with a pinch of salt." She picked up a glass and held it out for the server to fill it with the velvety, heady punch and just as he finished she exclaimed to Lady Margaret, "Oh, look, have you ever seen such a dreadful dress!" Amelia distracted her by pointing across the room and Lady Margaret quickly turned around to see what she was pointing at. In that brief moment, Amelia snatched up the salt pot and poured a healthy amount into the glass of punch.

By the time Lady Margaret turned back around looking a little puzzled, Amelia was serenely holding out a glass of punch and a glass of wine. "There you are. I sincerely hope you enjoy it."

"You are very thoughtful, my dear."

As she watched her weave her way back through the crowd, Amelia's face took on a look of pure devilment. That would teach the evil harlot a lesson.

She suddenly found a hand on her elbow and looked up to find Oliver staring down at her, his eyes full of suspicion. She felt her face flush hotly under his knowing gaze and her eyes widened a fraction but even so, she tried to muster up a semblance of normality. If he knew what she had done, she would be in a whole heap of trouble.

"Oh, Oliver, I was just deciding which pastries to bring back."

"Were you? Or were you up to no good?" he said, his voice low to avoid others overhearing.

"What do you mean?"

"You know very well. I know that look on your face and I can only surmise it to be directed at Lady Caroline somehow."

"Not at all. I dislike the woman but that's all. I was just smiling. Is that a crime?"

"Don't be facetious, Amelia." he admonished her. "I just saw you hand two drinks to Lady Margaret and when she walked away, you gave her a mischievous look."

Suddenly there was a commotion out in the foyer. Everyone looked over and began to jostle towards the door to see what was going on.

"Stand aside, if you please!" boomed a loud voice.

Oliver, having the advantage of being taller than most people, stared across the tops of their heads and frowned.

Amelia tugged on his sleeve. "What is it? What is happening?"

"I can't quite make it out. Wait here and I will go and see if assistance is needed."

He disappeared from her view and she was left, biting her lip. What if it was something to do with Lady Caroline? Oh dear. Had her prank backfired?

———— ⟨∾⟩ ————

Oliver made his way through the crowd until he found the cause of the commotion. He stood in the doorway of the ladies' parlour and could see that the main attention seemed to be focussed on Lady Caroline.

She was reclined upon the chaise longue, a damp cloth upon her head and wrist and appeared the picture of frailty - pale skin, heavy-lidded eyes, delicate frame trembling ever so slightly. Lady Margaret was standing to her side, rapidly wafting a fan over her face.

The local doctor was in attendance, taking her pulse with a concerned frown.

Oliver turned to a woman standing nearby. "May I ask, what has happened?"

"She is having a fit of the vapours, Sir. She is prone to them."

Another woman next to her started tutting at her condition. "What has caused this latest episode though?"

"I heard someone mention salt in her drink but I do wonder if that was her poor nerves making her nonsensical. I mean to say, why would there be salt in her drink?" The other woman said, looking skeptical.

"Indeed, that does seem a little far-fetched," Oliver muttered. But deep down he knew exactly who would have done such a thing. He diverted the attention away, "Perhaps her nerves were a little overwrought from all the people present. Too much noise, not enough oxygen, that sort of thing."

The woman nodded. "Oh, indeed. It can be a little overwhelming for someone with such a delicate disposition."

Delicate? Thought Oliver. There was nothing delicate about the spoiled Lady Caroline but those thoughts were best kept to himself.

He saw the doctor pat her hand and then he closed his medical bag, heading towards the exit. Oliver caught him as he left, "Is Lady Caroline recovered?"

"Yes, I have advised her to rest awhile and if she feels well enough, she can enjoy the rest of the evening."

"Someone mentioned her drink having salt in it? Is that correct?"

"It is true. I tasted it myself. It was only a harmless mistake or maybe a prank and I don't suppose we will ever find the culprit. But Lady Caroline, took rather a large gulp and the shock made her gag, poor woman. I think she thought she had been poisoned!"

"And that brought on an episode of her nerves."

The doctor nodded. "Indeed it did. But a little bit of rest and she will be fine."

"Thank you, doctor."

So now he knew what the devilish expression on his fiancée's face was about. With a determined expression he went in search of the wayward little madam for he had questions that needed to be answered!

Amelia had already taken flight and was thinking of hiding outside in the gardens. She had already heard the whispers that Lady Caroline was being attended to by the doctor and knew that when Oliver found out, then her backside was history!

He didn't miss a thing!

But her sister, Florence had waylaid her just as she was going to step outside. She was asking what to buy their Mama for her upcoming birthday. Amelia cursed inwardly, couldn't she have asked some other time? She listened to her talk, waiting for the moment she could high-tail it into the gardens. But it was not to be.

"Might I interrupt?" A deep voice at her side told her that Oliver had found her. She closed her eyes for a moment and then turned to look at him, her eyes wary. Did he suspect her? Please God, he didn't know. But his foreboding looks told her that he had. Oh, lord!

He turned to her sister. "I wonder, Mrs. Portman, if I might have a word with your sister in private?"

"Of course. I shall go and join my husband."

When she had disappeared into the crowd, Oliver turned back around and looked down at Amelia, his countenance stern. She asked tentatively, "Did you find out what the commotion was about?"

"Oh, yes. It would seem that someone had put salt in Lady Caroline's drink causing her to have a nervous breakdown. She is currently lying on a chaise longue recovering."

Amelia gulped, "Oh, dear me."

Although she was afeared of Oliver's wrath, she couldn't quite quell the bubble of laughter that threatened to break forth. Putting a hand over her mouth, she stifled a smile as she thought of Lady Caroline's predicament. It served her right.

"You find this funny?" Oliver said.

"No, no, or course not." She looked down at the ground and shuffled her feet nervously, her mirth rapidly disappearing.

"I see that once again I must take you to task." He placed a firm grip on her elbow and leaned in close to whisper in her ear, "Don't even think of lying to me. You and I both know that you were the culprit so I give you two choices. You can either come with me right this second and take your punishment or I can do it right here, right now, in front of the whole damn assembly because believe me, you will be punished one way or the other!"

Amelia's heart leapt and she pulled back, looking into his face. He was livid, his eyes glistening with anger. She had thought herself safe from his sharp hand in such a public place but it seemed she had been wrong. She swallowed hard and tried to reason with him.

"I meant no harm, Oliver. Truly, it was only intended as a bit of harmless fun. Can we not discuss this rather than you... you... "

He interrupted her immediately. "No, I intend to see that backside of yours is given a sound thrashing. You need to learn to behave."

"You are being unreasonable." She tried to shift backwards but his grip tightened.

"No, Amelia, I am not. Now is it to be here or elsewhere, because I am fast losing patience!"

Amelia glanced around at the throng of people and decided that under no circumstances was she going to be made a spectacle of. Perhaps once away from the main hall and somewhere quiet, she could either run away from him or try once again to make him see reason.

Licking her lips, she raised her chin and spoke quietly. "Very well, we shall go elsewhere."

Amongst the mass of people, their exit went unnoticed and it was with great trepidation that Amelia allowed him to lead her into the gardens and then further into a rather large walled garden for privacy.

Now they were alone, Amelia's stomach tightened and she tried to pull away, realizing that Oliver only had one intent – and that was not to reason. "You don't have to do this!"

"Oh, I do!" In one fell swoop, he had her pinned down over his lap, her skirts swept up over her back and one strong leg wrapped over both of hers, so she couldn't escape. "Your actions deserve nothing less!"

"No!" She kicked her legs but his powerful thigh prohibited any real movement. "Oh!"

His large hand made contact with her soft buttocks through the thin material of her bloomers and she shrieked with pain. "That hurts!"

"As I intend it to!"

She shivered as much from the angry tone in his voice, to the pain he was inflicting on her backside.

He began a steady rhythm, spank after spank, that soon had her begging for release. "Please, Oliver, it was only a prank! Ouch!" She yelped but still his hand came down. She tried protecting herself but quickly found her hand captured at the small of her back as he continued to mete out punishment on her backside.

"Stop it! Stop it!" she cried. "Aow!" She screwed her face up, trying to deal with the pain as his hand made contact with her now-throbbing flesh.

Her bottom was heating up like a furnace and the pain was becoming unbearable. His hand moved lower to her sit spots and smacked each cheek in turn several times.

Quickly, she realized that he wasn't going to stop until she was most contrite. "Please stop! I am truly sorry for my behaviour!"

He smacked her twice more and then pulled her up, but still kept a tight grip on her upper arm. "Didn't you realise how damaging that episode could have been to your reputation yet alone a scandal to your family's name?"

She shook her head and shuffled her feet.

"If you ever dare do such a thing again, I will see a cane taken to your backside and you will not sit for a week!"

She pouted and sent him a sullen look before rubbing her sore bottom better. Once again, she was in trouble with him. He placed his large hand under her chin and tilted her face so she had to look at him.

"Will you ever learn, I wonder, Amelia, or will you always have this stubborn streak that allows such wilful behaviour?"

"I am not wilful!"

"You are and when we are married I shall make sure that you understand how I expect my wife to behave."

Amelia's eyes widened, knowing he meant every word.

"Now we shall rejoin the ball and you, my little madam, will behave!"

Amelia huffed slightly but took his arm as he led her back through the gardens towards the hall. Her bottom ached with every step but she put on a brave face. She certainly didn't want anyone to find out what had just happened!

Especially not the odious Lady Caroline!

Chapter Nine

"Do you have to stand so close, Lord Pembley?" Lady Caroline snapped, glaring at him. She had finally recovered from her attack of nerves and was standing by the window, getting some air.

He immediately took a step backwards and trod straight on Lady Margaret's toes. She yelped and he apologised most profusely. "I do beg your pardon, Lady Margaret." Turning back to Lady Caroline he explained, "I am merely concerned for your well-being, my dear. I wish I had been here earlier to aid you in your malaise but my carriage was delayed."

Lady Caroline rolled her eyes. "There is no need to explain. Perhaps you could fetch me a glass of champagne?" It was more of an order than a request.

"Of course, my dear."

She watched him go and pulled a face. Why had she ever allowed him to court her in the first place? He had lots of money but that was all. He wasn't bad looking but certainly not as handsome or dashing as Lord Berkeley. Now there was a handsome man.

Thinking of him made her eyes narrow because it immediately conjured up an image of Amelia Roberts. What on earth did that devious girl have that she didn't? She wasn't even in the same class as herself.

She would bet she was behind that salt in her drink but she couldn't prove it. After all, she was the one that handed it to Lady Margaret.

But she had a mighty piece of information that would control that girl's future and at the first chance, she would put it into action.

Oh, yes, Amelia Roberts - your life was about to change for the worse!

Oliver was standing waiting to be served with a drink when Lord Pembley appeared at his side. They had been introduced earlier and Oliver had liked him on sight. A very affable fellow and only a little older than himself. At this precise moment though, he looked a little down hearted.

"How goes it, Lord Pembley?"

"Not very well, really." Lord Pembley's brow furrowed and it was clear something was troubling him.

"Could I be of assistance at all?" Oliver offered.

"Well, I don't know. My problem involves a woman."

Oliver nodded, "I see. Would it help to talk about it? We can retire to the cards room and speak privately if you like."

"I would like to hear your opinion and any advice would be most welcome but you are sure it won't inconvenience you?"

Oliver shook his head, "Not at all."

"Very well, I will meet you there in a moment just as soon as I have taken this glass of champagne to Lady Caroline. If I take too long she will be the first to moan!"

Oliver watched him go and raised an eyebrow. He'd give her something to moan about if she dared complain. A smacked bottom would set her right. Poor Lord Pembley. He was in for a tough marriage if he didn't learn to control her.

A little while later, Lord Pembley took a seat next to Oliver on one of the unoccupied gaming tables. The room was quite noisy and anything they had to say would be lost in the lively atmosphere.

Oliver listened sympathetically whilst Lord Pembley revealed his qualms about marrying Lady Caroline and her fiery nature.

"So what do you think I should do? I want to marry her but I fear her wicked tongue."

Oliver leaned back in his chair and thought about his own relationship. Amelia was a little rebel and he couldn't imagine letting her get away with any wayward behaviour. For one, his own sanity and secondly, her safety.

But marriage was a partnership and learning to live together and understand one another's limits required time.

"Lord Pembley, this is a very challenging subject indeed and it rather depends on how you see your relationship together."

"Yes, and I am truly confused about the whole issue."

"I think, personally, that she will have to learn to have more respect for your feelings. At the moment, she deems it acceptable to have the upper hand." He tapped his fingers on the table, "And if she continues, that will only breed resentment. I feel she should have more respect for you, if you don't mind me saying."

He waited to see how Lord Pembley reacted before continuing. It was, after all, a very sensitive subject.

"I agree with you, I really do but how does one earn the respect of such a strong willed woman? I dislike the way she speaks to me but I fear her rebuttable should I say anything to the contrary. I do love her, you know."

"Then you must either accept the way things are or take her to task."

Lord Pembley looked at him sharply, "How does one do that?"

"With a good old fashioned spanking, Lord Pembley. A good bottom warming before bed will have her rethinking her attitude rapidly."

"I could never do that!" He looked quite shocked but Oliver could see in his eyes that he had set his thoughts off on a path of new discovery.

"Well, Lord Pembley, if you would excuse me, I must return to my fiancée."

He left Lord Pembley mulling over his words. Whether he decided to take that path, only time would tell but one thing was for sure, if Lady Caroline was his betrothed she'd find herself straight over his knee!

T*he next day*
Amelia awoke the next morning and rolling over in bed, she remembered what had happened the day before. Oh lord. Was she always going to be in Oliver's bad books?

Her bottom was still a bit tender, those hands of his were like iron and no matter what he had said, she didn't think she had deserved such a harsh punishment.

Lady Caroline was mean to the core and she deserved what had happened. She smiled to herself. She would have liked to see her take a big gulp of the salty beverage. Imagine her face!

Anna bustled in with some hot water for her mornings ablutions. "Someone is looking very happy!" she noted.

Amelia laughed softly, "I was just thinking about yesterday. What a wonderful night it was."

"You can tell me about it whilst you get ready. Are you still intending to visit with Miss Spencer this morning? If so, I will get your riding habit ready."

"Oh, yes! I promised her I would tell her everything about the evening." Her face fell, "It is such a pity she couldn't come. She would have enjoyed it so much."

"Ah, it won't be long before she's up and about. Didn't the doctor say only another week's bedrest?" Anna reminded her.

"You are right, as always. I shall have a quick breakfast and ride over to Abbeyfield."

The morning air was filled with the fresh scents of new growth as Amelia cantered her mare Lily out of the wrought iron gates towards the lane. Her mother had tried to dissuade her from riding alone because of Rufus Armstrong but she had managed to ease her mind by saying that she would take one of the hunting dogs with her. Jasper was her favourite. He was loyal and very protective. If anyone dared to go near her, he'd have them in a heartbeat!

She cantered onwards, revelling in the peaceful sounds and sights of spring. All around, the hedgerows were bursting with pale buds swelling on branches still bare from winter's rest. It was her favourite time of year.

Despite all the beauty around her, there was one thing that Amelia couldn't ignore and that was her sore bottom. She shifted, trying to get comfortable but no amount of wriggling helped. Trust her to have a fiancé that spanked!

She rounded the bend and then pulled Lily to an abrupt halt. In the distance, she spotted blue uniforms darting among the trees. It was the police!

Abbeyfield wasn't far. What if they had come upon Rufus Armstrong? Her eyes widened. Jasper was standing to attention, his tail rigid and his eyes fixed on the men as they ran through the forest. The police had to be chasing someone. Why else would they be here?

Curiosity overcoming caution, Amelia dismounted and taking hold of Jasper's collar, she followed the sounds of rustling leaves and shouts on foot. Peering through the foliage, she glimpsed a man stumbling over roots in panic. Was it Rufus?

Before she could get a clearer look, Constable Atkins emerged beside her. "Best get back on your horse, miss," he warned. "There's a villain hereabouts and it is not a place for a young lady to be. We have almost got our man. You run along now!"

Amelia nodded and hurried back to Lily, but she had too many questions swirling in her mind.

With the faithful Jasper by her side, she remained where she was, letting Lily graze peacefully whilst she waited to see if the man they were chasing was Rufus. She had to see him captured for her own sake.

She didn't have to wait long. After a lot of shouting and whistle blowing, they finally caught the scoundrel. It was only when she saw him marched off that she let out a sigh of relief. Justice was being served at last. With Rufus captured, life could return to normal, especially for her dear friend Cora.

Mounting Lily, she rode the rest of the way to Abbeyfield with more news to tell Cora than she could have imagined.

— ⟲ —

A little while later at Abbeyfield, Amelia recounted her findings to an eager Cora.

"Oh my!" she gasped. "Is it finally over?"

Amelia nodded, "I am so relieved!"

"As am I!" Cora covered her cheeks and closed her eyes. "These last few weeks have been hellish!" She opened them again and clasped Amelia's hand. "I cannot thank you enough, you are such a dear friend."

Amelia grinned, "Well you could always take me to the tea rooms and treat me to one of those delicious apple tartlets!" she patted her hand, "When you are recovered of course!"

"The doctor says that maybe tomorrow I can start walking around the gardens. I only have a twinge of pain now and that is nothing to what it was." She grimaced, "I cannot wait to get out and about again!"

"And I cannot wait either. The weather is improving and we have many paths and fields to explore! The best of summer is yet to come and we shall enjoy them together."

"What about your fiancé?" Cora said, grinning at her. "Will he object?"

"No! Of course not. He loves you just as much as I do. We shall enjoy the summer together, the three of us!"

"Have you set a date for the wedding yet?" Cora asked excitedly.

"Oh, good lord no. We have only just told my parents of his intentions to court me. There is plenty of time for that. Now, as you are still unfortunately bedridden, you might want to hear the next chapter in my little book." Amelia shot her a saucy grin.

"Oh, absolutely!" Cora grinned, "I am always eager for that!"

Smiling wickedly, Amelia pulled open the book and, finding the correct page, began to read to a very attentive audience.

That afternoon

Oliver was just coming out of the mercantile store in town when he came across Constable Atkins.

"Ah, Constable Atkins, I was going to come and see you later. I wondered if you had thought any more about Mr. Roberts and I joining you on the stakeout?"

Constable Atkins touched his hat. "No need, m'lord. Reckon the folk around here can rest a bit easier tonight for we have finally caught the scoundrel!"

"Is that so?" Oliver replied, raising an eyebrow with interest. "That blackmailing blighter is no longer free. How did you manage to apprehend him?"

The constable grinned with satisfaction. "Well, I had my suspicions he'd be lurking around Abbeyfield, so I laid in wait with my men. Sure enough, we found him prowling around in the woods and that's when we pounced. Took him completely by surprise!"

"Well done, Constable, well done indeed!" laughed Oliver, clapping the man on the back. "With that rascal behind bars where he belongs, the town can rest easy once more. My compliments to you and your men for a job well done."

"Thank you kindly, m'lord. Just doing my duty." And with another tip of his hat, Constable Atkins took his leave, riding high on the pride of a mission successfully accomplished.

Lady Caroline was still in high dudgeon. Just the mere thought of Amelia Roberts made her blood boil. Her eyes narrowed as her temper threatened to overwhelm her.

Why should she ensnare someone as handsome as Lord Berkeley. It just wasn't fair. She could see she was pretty but so was she herself! And more to the point, she had a title, Amelia did not! She sighed crossly.

But she wasn't completely deluded. When she had spoken with Lord Berkeley she had seen the look of derision in his eyes. He had no more need of her than she had of Lord Pembley. She silently admonished herself. Lord Pembley wasn't so bad, she just wished he was more masterful.

Well, if she couldn't have Lord Berkeley then she was going to make damned sure, Amelia Roberts wasn't going to have him either. She knew her secret and after luncheon, she was going to take her carriage into nearby Chatham and visit Lord Berkeley at his home. No one took advantage of Lady Caroline without consequences!

Bedford Hall

Oliver had just stepped out of the bath when Fletcher arrived with a fresh towel. "My lord, there is a Lady Caroline Egerton to see you."

Oliver's good mood rapidly disappeared. What the devil was she doing here? He took the towel off Fletcher and said, "Show her into the parlour and tell her I will attend her shortly."

As he dried himself he tried to think why she would pay him a visit. She never had before. It was most odd and knowing her personality, he knew it didn't bode well. Maybe she had discovered that his fiancée had tampered with her drink at the ball?

Lady Caroline was standing by the window in the parlour looking out across the grounds, when he entered the room.

"Good afternoon, Lady Caroline. I am a little surprised to see you here? For what do I owe the pleasure?" He kept his voice polite but wary.

"My lord, I simply must speak with you at once," she said in hushed tones.

"Oh? What about?"

He watched her and realised she was putting on a performance. She was wicked to the core and it was quite obvious she was about to cause trouble.

She sighed dramatically and raising her eyes to his, she said, "It is about Miss Roberts, my lord. I fear there is something amiss that you ought to know, though it near breaks my heart to be the bearer of such news."

Of course it does, he thought to himself, knowing full well she was hoping to create a divide. Gesturing for her to sit down, he poured a glass of sherry. "I can tell you are quite distressed. Perhaps you should drink this before you say anymore."

After taking a fortifying sip, Lady Caroline laid a hand over her heart. "During my visit to Miss Spencer's house a few weeks ago, I happened to overhear an exchange between her and your fiancée. I hardly dare tell you for it is such a scandalous affair."

Oliver's eyes narrowed and he rubbed his forehead, trying to suppress an irritated sigh. "Please, do continue."

"I thought it only fair you know, before you commit your future to hers unwittingly. But Miss Spencer was being blackmailed and your fiancée went and actually met the man face to face and paid him money!"

Lord Berkeley frowned heavily. "I see."

"You-you don't seem shocked?" she said, searching his face. "Did you know about this?"

"Did you think I wouldn't?" He said sternly, "You came here today to deliberately cause trouble, didn't you?"

"I don't know what you mean!" she blustered, her cheeks growing red.

"Oh, yes you do."

Lady Caroline jumped up from the seat, her eyes flashing with indignation. Now the game was up her true nature came to the fore. "I don't want you to marry, Miss Roberts! In fact, I forbid it! If you don't break off your engagement I will see to it that everyone knows the truth regarding Miss Spencer and Rufus Armstrong! And also your fiancée's involvement!"

"No one will believe you." He stated calmly, which seemed to incense her even more.

She balled her fists at her sides, "Oh yes they will! Everyone is afeared of the horrible man and when they find out that not only is he a pick-pocket but he has been dallying with Miss Spencer, well, I hate to think of the scandal that would ensue!"

Oliver stroked his chin, deep in thought, wondering how to handle the harpy in front of him. She truly needed taking in hand.

He walked over to her and folding his arms over his broad chest, he gave her a hard stare. "I think, if I were you, I wouldn't say another word."

She stared at him angrily and went to open her mouth. So he raised his finger, "Not another word! You will sit there and hear me out."

She must have heard the anger in his tone for she reluctantly obeyed him.

"You profess to despise Rufus Armstrong for blackmailing Miss Spencer yet here you are, trying to blackmail me. Do you honestly think that I would call off a marriage to the woman I love because of your threats? Do you think me so weak that I would bow down to your wishes?" He leaned in to her and she sank back into the chair.

"For your information, Rufus Armstrong was arrested this morning and is no longer a threat. So your words are empty, Lady Caroline."

"You lie!"

"No, I never lie." His eyes threatened her to challenge him. "If you were mine, I would give you a damned good spanking for your behaviour tonight!"

"Well, I have never been spoken to...!"

He interrupted her, "Well it is about time you were taken in hand, Lady Caroline. You are spoiled beyond reason!"

She jumped up from the chair and stormed from the room without another word.

Oliver watched the door slam shut and shook his head. What a horrible woman. Thank goodness Rufus was behind bars.

He had a good mind to inform Lord Pembley about her behaviour. In fact, he most definitely would. He would refrain from saying the exact details but it might be the impetus Lord Pembley needed to take the woman in hand and actually inflict some authority. He may even spank the harpy. Oh, he would like to be a fly on the wall to hear her wails!

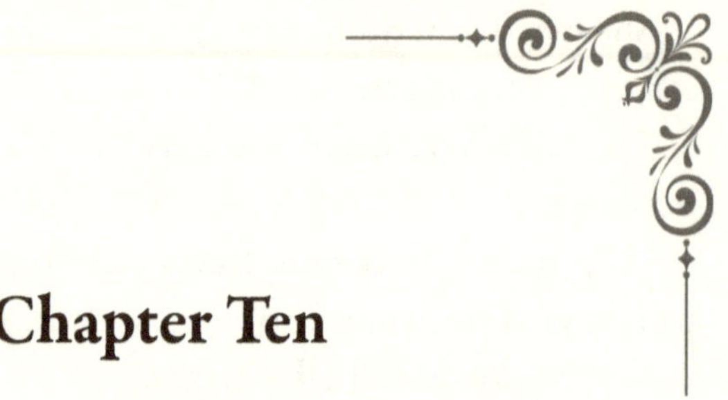

Chapter Ten

A*few days later*

Oliver strode into the Rose and Crown inn, eyes scanning the dim common room until he spied his friend Clarence tucked away in a corner.

"Lord Oliver, over here!" Clarence called with a wave.

Oliver made his way over, greeting Clarence warmly before signaling to the serving girl. As he sat down, another familiar face caught his eye across the room. It was Lord Pembley.

He had been mulling over whether or not to inform him about Lady Caroline and had come to the firm decision that it would be in everyone's favour if he revealed what she had done. He wouldn't tell him names as such, just the events and then it would be left up to Lord Pembley as to how he would act upon the information. He certainly knew what he would do!

"Clarence, I just need a quick word with Lord Pembley. I won't be long."

"Oh? Anything I need to know?" He raised an eyebrow, his curiosity piqued.

Oliver shook his head and patted him on the shoulder. "No, nothing you need concern yourself about."

He made his way over to Lord Pembley's table and said, "Lord Pembley, I wonder, could I join you for a moment?"

Lord Pembley obliged and with a warm smile, offered him the seat opposite. Oliver came straight to the point, "I had rather an unsettling encounter with Lady Caroline a few days ago and I feel the need to inform you. As difficult as it is, I think it best you know."

Lord Pembley frowned, "I am not certain I am going to like what you have to say."

Oliver sighed. "Be that as it may, will you hear me out?"

"Yes, of course I will."

"I cannot tell you the full details as I wish to keep certain parties' identities concealed but I can tell you that Lady Caroline overheard a conversation and thought to use it against me."

Lord Pembley's jaw dropped. "Was she snooping?"

"It does seem that way. Which in itself is not so bad but to use that information to blackmail me, is beyond comprehension."

"Blackmail you say? Good lord!"

Oliver related his tale but left out names and by the time he had finished, Lord Pembley was sitting there in shock.

"I don't take any pleasure in being the harbinger of such news," Oliver assured him, "but I think it only right that you know what happened."

Lord Pembley's eyes widened in disbelief. "But how could this be? Lady Caroline has a sharp tongue but has always appeared loyal and devoted. Are you certain of this accusation?"

Oliver nodded grimly. "Absolutely. I am sorry I had to bring you such news but it is now up to you, how you act upon it. I wish you well and in parting, I would say, remember my advice from the other night. It may be something to keep in mind when you confront Lady Caroline."

Lord Pembley nodded slowly and, emitting a long sigh, he said, "Well, I am very glad you told me, Lord Berkeley."

Oliver left him sitting at the table. That was one of the hardest things he had ever done but it had to be said. Joining Clarence, he picked up his glass of port and pushed Lady Caroline from his mind.

It was now Lord Pembley's problem. One minx on his hands was quite enough for him!

L ord Pembley's residence
     The crackling fire in Lord Pembley's study cast an amber glow upon the room, illuminating the tension that hung heavy in the air. Lord Pembley sat at his desk, tapping his fingers on the polished wooden surface, his expression serious, his body tense. The time had come for him to confront Lady Caroline about her scandalous behaviour and even though he knew what he had to do, it didn't come easily.

A soft knock on the study door interrupted his thoughts, and he called out, "Enter."

Lady Caroline, dressed in an elegant gown, swept into the room like she always did with a mix of arrogance and disdain in her eyes. She glanced at Lord Pembley expecting him to greet her with dereference but he didn't move.

An irritated frown marred her brow, "You don't seem particularly happy to see me, Lord Pembley. Is something amiss?"

He clasped his hands together and stared at her. "Yes, there is. I happened to speak with Lord Berkeley yesterday and he had some very interesting information for me."

He noted her expression had changed and she looked quite startled, "Oh?"

He kept his voice cold and measured as he replied, "Lady Caroline, I have just learned of your attempt to blackmail him. Is this true?"

Her eyes grew wide and he could tell she was suddenly nervous. So it was true, he thought! Her face paled and she sat down in the chair opposite. "Of course it isn't true!" she finally gasped, "I cannot believe you would even think I could do such a thing!"

"Lady Caroline, do you truly wish to become my wife?"

Her eyes darted to his and he could see she was trying to compose herself before replying, "Well, we are engaged so naturally I…"

"Yes, but do you love me?" he interrupted her. "Because there is only one way we can move forward in this relationship and that will be when you reveal the truth. I want to hear your side of the story and if you lie, I will put you straight over my knee."

She gasped loudly and jumped up from her seat. "Did you… did you just threaten to spank me?"

He nodded calmly. He had thought he wouldn't be able to carry out this role but now he was living it, he found it came quite naturally. And in all truth, what he had told her was true. If she didn't confess to her crime, then he had no desire to marry her at all.

He watched her chest rise and fall as she tried to compose herself. Would she stay or would she go?

She took a deep breath and sat back down in the chair, her usual haughty pose nowhere to be seen, "Yes, it is true. But please understand, I was desperate and misguided. I never intended for things to escalate this far."

Lord Pembley, his voice tinged with reproval, replied, "Desperation is no excuse for such behaviour, Lady Caroline. You are lucky that Lord Berkeley is a man of such standing and forgiveness."

Her eyes welled up with tears, more than likely from self-pity rather than her actions but it was a start. Her voice wavering, she said quietly, "I deeply regret my actions. I was overcome with hatred for Miss Roberts and I should never ever have said those things. Will you forgive me?"

Lord Pembley stood, his voice firm. "Thank you for your honesty, Lady Caroline. What you did was wrong but I will forgive you this time. Just understand that if you ever do anything like this again, I will surely carry out my threat."

Lady Caroline's eyes widened and he saw within their shining depths, a hint of humility. It heartened him no end. With her voice unusually subdued, she said, "I understand, Lord Pembley. I will accept whatever consequences come my way and... and I am truly sorry for the pain I have caused."

"Well then, let us start afresh." He held out his arm, "We shall take a walk in the gardens and forget any of this happened."

As they left the study, Lord Pembley couldn't help but marvel at the change in his fiancée. Lord Berkeley certainly knew a thing or two about handling women!

⁓⟡⁓

A week later, Rufus Armstrong's trial captivated the attention of the town. Witnesses came forward, relaying their encounters with the notorious pickpocket. The evidence against Rufus was overwhelming, leaving little doubt in the minds of the jury.

Oliver attended the hearing and was relieved that there was enough evidence to bring the man to justice without ever having to reveal Miss Spencer's involvement with the scoundrel.

The courtroom was filled with anticipation as the judge delivered the verdict. "Rufus Armstrong, you have been found guilty of pickpocketing and theft," the judge declared, his voice echoing through the grand chamber. "You shall be remanded in custody and serve your sentence accordingly."

Oliver took much delight when he saw Rufus's shoulders slump, his once confident demeanor replaced with a sense of resignation. He was led away, the heavy doors of the courtroom closing behind him, sealing his fate.

⁓⟡⁓

Evesham Manor

The sun was warm but not oppressive as Oliver strolled among the bright blooms of Evesham Manor's gardens with Amelia beside him. It was now early June and the flowers were in full glorious display.

Delicate roses adorned the trellises, their light perfume pervading the air in the gentle breeze.

Oliver had suggested the gardens as he wanted privacy for the important matter he wanted to discuss.

Reaching one of the stone benches, he drew Amelia down next to him and held her hand. She looked up at him, a smile playing on her face. She was so beautiful.

"My love," Oliver began, his voice steady, "We have been courting for nearly three months now and in all truth, I cannot bear to wait any longer. Will you have me for your husband?" He lifted her hand and kissed her soft knuckles, "And set a date for the wedding?"

Amelia's eyes widened a little and she paused before replying with a mischievous grin, "Well, Lord Oliver, I am still uncertain that I wish to have a husband that spanks me."

He could see she was playing with him, so he replied in kind, "Then all you have to do is learn to behave, my little madam. Is it so hard?"

Before she had a chance to reply, he pulled her against him and captured her lips, softly at first and then with more fervor. She responded passionately as she always did which was why he couldn't wait any longer to truthfully make her his.

When they broke apart her eyes were glazed with passion and she breathed, "How can I say no to a man who kisses like you do!"

Relief and elation flooded Oliver's being, his heart soaring with joy. She might be rebellious on occasion and need disciplining but that was why she needed someone strong like him. Someone to care for her and keep her safe.

Sweeping her into his arms once more, he kissed her soundly knowing that soon she would be his completely.

A *month later...*

The small chapel on the estate was filled with a sense of anticipation and reverence as family and friends gathered to witness the union of Lord Oliver Berkeley and Miss Amelia Roberts in holy matrimony.

Amelia was incredibly nervous but excited all at the same time. So much so that she thought she would burst! She glanced around the chapel, it had been beautifully decorated with delicate lace and ribbons, transforming it into a vision of beauty. Bouquets of fragrant flowers adorned the altar, their vibrant hues lending a touch of nature's splendor to the sacred space.

She looked down at her dress. It was a vision of ivory and cream lace that cascaded elegantly around her. Her veil, adorned with delicate pearls, framed her face and trailed half way down her back.

Oliver was standing next to her and he had never looked so handsome. He was dressed in a dashing formal morning suit, accompanied by a crisp white shirt and a cravat.

The reverend cleared his throat to capture her attention and wide eyed she listened as he began the ceremony, his voice resonating throughout the chapel.

Vows were exchanged and when the reverend pronounced them husband and wife, the guests erupted into cheers and applause, their joy filling the sacred space. Amelia looked over at her mother and saw her dabbing at her eyes with a small hanky. Even her father didn't look quite as stern as usual.

She turned to look at her husband, happiness and love clearly visible on his face and when he drew her gently towards him and sealed their union with a tender kiss, she knew she had made the right decision.

As they walked down the aisle, hand in hand, petals rained down upon them, thrown by exuberant guests. The chapel doors opened wide, revealing the sunlit countryside beyond, and

they began the short walk to the main house to have the reception.

At the end of the meal and before the dancing was due to begin, Cora drew her aside. "You look simply stunning, Amelia. I am so thrilled for you, truly. I think that you and Lord Berkeley make such a handsome couple."

"Oh, that's such a lovely thing to say, Cora."

"And it is the absolute truth." She grinned, "Oh, that I can find someone so eligible!"

"It won't be long I am sure. I intend to have many parties at Bedford Hall and when I do, you shall be the first to be invited. I will ask Lord Oliver to invite his friends. I am sure that amongst them you will find someone suitable."

"That sounds so exciting." Her expression suddenly changed and she exclaimed, "Oh, I forgot to tell you that Lady Caroline came to call the other day."

Amelia immediately pulled a face. "Oh, I pity you."

"No, it wasn't like usual. She was actually quite nice. It sounds odd for me to say that but it was true. Her manner was quite different."

"Why do you think that was?"

"I have no idea although she did keep speaking about her fiancé, Lord Pembley, in an almost reverent manner. Do you think he has something over her? I mean, she never used to talk about him like that. In fact, I think she quite despised him."

Amelia raised an eyebrow, "One never knows what skeletons that harpy might keep in her closet!"

They laughed wickedly.

Oliver joined them and slipped his arm around his wife's waist. "What are you two laughing about?" His eyes crinkled at their infectious laughter.

Amelia told him about the change in Lady Caroline's behaviour and he nodded with satisfaction.

Amelia immediately narrowed her eyes and asked, "What do you know that we don't?"

"That discussion, my sweet little wife, is for another day. At the moment, I believe you owe me a dance?"

Amelia soon found herself on the dance floor, wrapped in the arms of the man she loved and all thoughts of Lady Caroline were dismissed from her mind. Her life with her new husband was far too precious to waste time on someone so contemptible!

As he spun her around the dance floor he smiled down at her, his eyes sparkling with love and desire. This was all she needed.

That night

After a day filled with joy and celebration, Lord Oliver and Lady Amelia retired to the opulent chambers of Bedford Hall, having chosen to take the carriage the short ride home rather than stay at Evesham. For his first night alone with his winsome wife, Oliver wanted privacy.

He stepped out of the carriage first and turning around, took Amelia's hand but before her feet could touch the ground, he quickly swept her up in his arms. She giggled and put her arms around his neck.

"Why, Lord Oliver, what do you do?"

"It is customary to carry the bride over the threshold and that is exactly what I intend to do!"

Striding up the large stone steps, he was greeted at the top by Fletcher as he opened the wide polished oak door for them. "Good evening, my Lord, my Lady. Congratulations to you both."

"Good evening, Fletcher and thank you." Oliver said.

"Everything is prepared as you requested, my Lord."

"Excellent, then you may retire for the night."

Oliver carried Amelia through the hallway and then up the large winding staircase towards their bedroom. Bedford Hall was a grand manor with tastefully decorated interiors and upon entering the bedroom, Amelia was impressed at how Oliver's servants had prepared the room for them. It was beautiful.

The large, canopied bed was draped in luxurious silk and strewn with rose petals. Soft candlelight flickered, casting a warm and intimate glow upon the room. It was most welcoming but Amelia couldn't help but feel a little nervous about their first night together.

Placing her down on the bed, Oliver told her not to move. A few moments later he returned with a glass of champagne each. She sat up and took the offered glass, smiling shyly at him.

Clinking glasses, he said, "To our first night together, my love."

She took a sip of the sparkling drink and felt the heady liquid course through her veins, calming her nerves.

With a tender gesture, Oliver raised his hand and carefully untied the ribbons and pins that held her hair in place, allowing the locks to spill freely, tumbling about her slender shoulders.

She felt his fingers slip through the golden tendrils and he commented, softly, "Your hair is like spun silk.'

Amelia sighed contentedly, her eyes closing momentarily as Oliver's touch sent a delightful shiver down her spine. She leaned into his gentle caress, savoring the tenderness and love that flowed through his fingertips.

O liver wanted his wife's first time to be as perfect as possible. Taking the half empty glass from her small hand, he slowly began to undress her, kissing her skin softly as it was exposed to his gaze.

She was perfection. Her flawless skin like alabaster.

"You have nothing to fear, my love. I will be gentle." He spoke gently, his voice thick with passion as he repeatedly kissed her neck and shoulder before moving upwards.

Her lips parted softly as his mouth found hers, his tongue finding its way into her mouth and fencing with her own as he coaxed a response from her.

Amelia was filled with desire as his lips blazed a trail of fire from her mouth down to her neck. He stroked the length of her, his hands closing over her breasts. Her nipples hardened when his mouth closed over them, one after the other, the peaks darkening to crimson as he tormented them with his tongue.

Of their own volition, Amelia's hands grasped his head. He moved lower, his tongue laving her abdomen. His large hands parted her thighs and Amelia gasped, a startled cry escaping her lips, as she felt his tongue sear her womanhood.

Oliver gently but firmly pushed her hands aside as she tried to resist. She moaned softly when he found her little nub of desire and began a steady assault, his hands kneading her bottom as his mouth teased her relentlessly. He felt her whole body tense and listened with pleasure to the soft cries that fell from her lips as she arched her back with desire.

Slowly, he made his way back up to her face, kissing and licking her gorgeous body as he went.

He kissed her on the mouth again, only this time harder, deeper, driven by an insatiable passion, as he supported his body by sliding his arm beneath her neck. With his other hand, he guided himself to her moist, velvet-like labia. He could never remember being this hard in his entire life and it was with this in mind that he gently began to enter her.

He felt her tense, "Oliver!"

"Hush, my love." He whispered as he gently filled her, inch by powerful inch, to get her used to his size until he felt the barrier signifying her virginity. He spoke softly to reassure her, "The pain will not last long."

His lips claimed hers before she could speak any further and he thrust himself inside to the hilt, muting her cries of pain as he broke through her maidenhead. She wrapped her arms around his neck and held on tightly as he began a rhythmic thrusting, his lips clamped to her own.

It wasn't long before Amelia's pain subsided, and to her amazement, she could feel her body begin to soar once again. Her muscles tightened and her heartbeat raced until just as she thought she would die, a thousand stars exploded around her.

Oliver wrapped his arms around her, thrusting into her with a driving force as he neared his own relief.

Amelia felt her body responding to her husband's and when he released inside her, she soared to new heights once again.

It was heavenly.

Oliver fell beside her, pulling her close. They remained silent for a while, both relaxing in the warm aftermath of their delicious lovemaking. Finally, he hoisted himself up onto one elbow and looked down into her face.

"I hope I didn't hurt you, my love."

She looked at him softly, "The pain was brief but afterwards, it was wonderful!"

Her eyes took on a soft hue as she remembered again the pleasure he had given her. Their lovemaking had far exceeded her expectations and she smiled happily to herself. Oliver had been so thoughtful and caring throughout ensuring her first time was as enjoyable as could be.

Rolling onto her side, she kissed his cheek. "I am so happy that you are my husband."

Capturing her hand, he raised it and kissed the soft skin, "And I am a very lucky man."

He pulled the covers up and drew her to him once more. Amelia snuggled up to his muscular body and with a soft sigh, her eyes fluttered closed and she fell asleep, safe in the arms of her handsome husband.

The end.

About the Author

Maryse Dawson was born in England but now lives in western France with her family - a husband, three children and two cats. When she's not writing she spends her time visiting the beaches and surrounding countryside. She has always enjoyed reading romances and loves history so began writing a few years ago to include domestic discipline in her stories. An alpha male - a feisty woman and adventures that will keep you turning the pages!

Read more at https://www.facebook.com/maryse.dawson.5.